Lost Embrace

Immortals of New Orleans, Book 6.5

Kym Grosso

MT Carvin Publishing, LLC
West Chester, Pennsylvania

Editor: Julie Roberts
Formatting: Polgarus Studio
Cover Design: LM Creations
Photographer: Golden Czermak
Cover Models: Justin Keeton & Tamara Summers

DISCLAIMER

This book is a work of fiction. The names, characters, locations and events portrayed in this book are a work of fiction or are used fictitiously. Any similarity to actual events, locales, or real persons, living or dead, is coincidental and not intended by the author.

NOTICE

This is an adult erotic paranormal romance book with love scenes and mature situations. It is only intended for adult readers over the age of 18.

ACKNOWLEDGMENTS

~My husband, Keith, for encouraging me to write and supporting me in everything I do.

~Julie Roberts, editor, who spent hours reading, editing and proofreading Lost Embrace. You've done so much to help and encourage me over the past two years. As with every book, I could not have done this without you!

~My Alpha readers, Rochelle and Maria, who help give me such important feedback and insight during the editing process. You both are awesome!

~My dedicated beta readers, Elena, Gayle, Denise, Janet, Jessica, Jerri, Leah, Laurie, Stephanie, and Rose for beta reading. I really appreciate all the valuable feedback you provide.

~LM Creations, cover artist, for cover design.

~Golden Czermak, for image and photography.

~Justin Keeton & Tamara Summers, cover models.

~Nicole, Indie Sage PR, for helping me with promotion and supporting my books.

~Gayle, my admin, who is one of my biggest supporters

and helps to run my street team. I'm so thankful for all of your help!

~My awesome street team, for helping spread the word about the Immortals of New Orleans series and my new erotic contemporary romance Altura series. I appreciate your support more than you could know! You guys are the best. You rock!

⤜❦· *Chapter One* ·❦⤛

The demon gored its claw into her belly, boring through her organs. She fell to the ground, and the thump of her skull cracking on the pavement reverberated in her ears. The black tunnel closed in as the beast spat into her wound, its acidic saliva burning her flesh. Clutching the cavernous gash, her bloodstained hands slipped from her skin as the life drained out of her.

Never wanting to be vampire, her love of her humanity had superseded all else. Despite having been guaranteed immortality by her vampire lover, she learned that such promises were relative to the manner of death. Though age and disease would not come for her, the demon's talons would prove to be fatal. Unlike everything she'd been told about death, her life didn't flash before her eyes. Only *he* was omnipresent in her thoughts. With her last breath, she called for him to save her. *Kade.* She'd always been a fighter until her final moment when hope was lost. As light turned to darkness, she accepted the inevitable. Giving in to death's embrace, she smiled, knowing that she'd loved, was loved.

Sydney braced for the seizure, her body tensing, readying for the barrage of spasms it would endure. It had been a month since she'd been attacked. She'd been protecting an innocent child from the monstrous demon who sought to claim her. As a police officer, it wasn't the first time she'd been in danger. But that day, she'd been no match for the evil beast who impaled her with his fist. As death reached for her soul, her fiancé, Kade Issacson, had saved her from its finality. Turned her without consent.

Sydney loved Kade more than life itself, but they'd always had an understanding; she'd remain human. She'd agreed to drink miniscule amounts of his blood, allowing her the benefits of immortality. As Kade's singular source of sustenance, she'd always known that if she were to be turned, he wouldn't be able to feed from her. Having been transformed into a vampire, no longer could she serve that role in his life. In the blink of an eye, her life had been destroyed, promises crushed.

The first round of chills racked her body, and she bit her lip raw. She curled into the corner of the room, the hardwood floor grounding her. She'd watched through the window as the donor approached the house. A healthy pink tinge on the woman's cheeks told her she'd rushed to her appointment. Even though Sydney knew Kade wouldn't partake of the stranger's blood, it didn't matter. Jealousy clutched at her gut. He'd feed eventually…sometime, somewhere, from someone else…but never from her. He'd need a human, and human she was not.

A tear rolled down her cheek as her muscles relaxed. She and Kade had barely spoken over the past month. She knew he loved her, had done what he thought needed to be done. Yet being turned had rocked her world, shattering the delicate life they'd built together.

Weak, she had been unable to feed without causing the donors excruciating pain. It was as if her fangs were intoxicated with the demon itself. Screaming herself awake had become the only relief from her nightmares of the beast. She'd convinced herself that Rylion had infected her with his saliva. Now her own fluids had brought terror to anyone she'd touched.

When Kade brought donors to her, Sydney would wait for him to sink his teeth into their wrist. She'd be forced to watch the woman shake with desire caused by her lover. At one time, his bite was meant only for her. On this dark night, however, another stranger would quiver at his touch.

A knock sounded before the doorknob creaked. Sydney shoved herself to her feet, and found a chair. Wiping the tears from her face, she took a deep breath, trying to find the courage to proceed. She struggled with thoughts of suicide, yet today the fight to survive prevailed. Reluctantly she'd accept the nourishment.

"Sydney, are you ready for us?" she heard Kade ask. The door edged open an inch.

"Yes," she whispered.

Her eyes met Kade's as he walked into her bedroom. A rush of excitement filled her belly as he came into view.

His blond hair had grown long, its shaggy edges brushing his collar. Sydney found his permanent five o'clock shadow every bit as sexy as his usual clean-shaven face. She wished she could hate him, leave him, but the deep burning love in her heart never ceased. It tore her apart to know she'd never be what he needed.

"Love, it's okay," he said, his warm voice attempting to calm her.

A petite blonde followed behind him. She knelt before Sydney and presented her arm in silence. Sydney glanced at her for only a second before meeting Kade's gaze. She fought the moisture that brimmed in her eyes.

"We'll do this quickly," Kade promised.

"It's okay," she lied.

"Hey." Kade cradled her face with his palms, his thumbs gently brushing the tears away. "I love you. We're going to figure this out. I promise you."

When he told her he loved her, it broke her heart. Sydney's gaze fell to the floor, unable to look at him. His warm lips grazed over hers, and she swallowed the soft cry that bubbled inside her throat. As his hands fell from her skin, she gazed out the window. She wished she could pretend to be blind to his actions. She refused to watch his fangs descend, but the sigh of the donor's arousal rang in her ears. Sydney thought she'd die another death, her chest heavy with emotion. By the time the blood hit her lips, she'd made a decision. She knew he wouldn't agree, but it was of little consequence. One way or another, it was time to regain control of her life.

Chapter Two

Kade snatched a bottle of scotch off the bar and fell back into his leather chair. He recalled the debacle of a feeding that had just played out with Sydney. He'd bitten into the strange woman, her blood like paint thinner on his tongue. In turn, Sydney had barely been able to choke down more than a few drops, and still wasn't nourished.

Kade cursed the fucking demon that had stolen Sydney's spirit. As she'd lain dying on the sidewalk, he hadn't thought twice about turning her. He'd known the consequences, but like a doctor performing an amputation, he'd chosen to cut off the limb to save a life. In the process, he'd killed the human within the woman he loved.

He'd known it would be difficult for Sydney to accept her new lifestyle. But he'd anticipated that in time she'd grow to understand that it was a matter of existence. He'd explained several times that the sexual feelings induced by their bite was necessary, a survival mechanism for the vampire race.

Footsteps in the hallway thwarted his racing thoughts and alerted him to the fact that he wasn't alone. His best friend, Luca Macquarie, stood watching him, his arm braced on the doorjamb. He'd known Luca would come, sensing his discontent.

"Scotch?" Kade poured a drink and slid a tumbler across his desk.

"Is that a question or an order?" Luca approached and took a seat.

"I'm running out of time." He held up his glass to the light, studying the amber legs trailing down the sides.

"We've got nothing but time, my friend."

"Not her."

"Did she feed?"

"What do you think?" Kade locked his tired eyes on Luca's.

"Is that a no?"

"She ate…barely. She's unable to control her bite."

"Still causing pain?"

"Tried it two days ago."

"And?"

"Let's just say I had to bite the donor a second time just to take the edge off her screaming. Needless to say, she won't be back."

"Can't you just continue as is? You bite the donor then she feeds?"

"Let me ask you this." Kade took a deep draw of the liquor, his lips drawn tight. "How would Samantha feel if you bit another woman? Another man for that matter?

Had to rely on someone else for food?"

"She'd hate it. Look, I see your point, but you're running out of options here." Luca rimmed the edge of his drink with his forefinger. "What's the great one say?"

Kade gave a small smirk, realizing Luca was referring to Léopold, the ancient vampire who'd turned him.

"Léopold believes it's psychological but won't rule out the possibility that the demon somehow mutated her. If that's true, she'll never be able to feed on her own…not bite easily, anyway. The human will struggle. Every time would be torture. She could end up killing them."

"Okay, well, let's assume the former, shall we? Have you tried male donors? It could give her an incentive…you know…make things more pleasurable for her."

"Yes," Kade bit out. The male had been every bit of a disaster as the woman.

"I take that it didn't go well."

"That would be correct. Not to mention that I know for damn sure you wouldn't want your woman's mouth on another man." Kade plowed his fingers through his hair. "I don't know…it's not that I'm opposed to her eating from a man per se, but it was just all wrong. I didn't know the donor. She didn't know him either. Learning how to control the pleasure without it turning sexual is an acquired skill."

"You let me bite her," Luca noted, averting his gaze.

"*She* let you feed from her. Once. To save your ass. And if you recall correctly, I told you that I wouldn't share her again," Kade replied.

"Yes, I do, but now you may have to do the same to save her."

"I'm not sure what you're implying."

"Let her feed from someone she knows. Samantha is pregnant so that's out but perhaps one of the wolves…"

"Maybe. I'd have to ask the Alpha."

"Think about it…their blood is strong. The Alpha's mate, Wynter, she would be a good choice. She's a woman. And she and Sydney are friends. The Alpha owes you this anyway. Sydney ended up in this predicament saving her and their child."

"Wolves aren't our usual food source."

"Who then? Does she have any other human friends who are willing?" Luca asked.

"She hasn't been down here very long. She doesn't know many people," Kade hedged. "I've got to do something, though. I'm losing her."

"You're not losing her."

"I am. I can see the desperation in her eyes. Some days," Kade pinched the bridge of his nose, "she's not fighting. That day I saved her, I think she was ready to die. I mean, despite everything I could give her, her job had certain dangers. Dying…she knew it was a possibility. She always told me that she wanted to stay human. She was my mortal, and now…things are changed. We must rely on others for blood. She can't handle me feeding from another woman. And fuck, I can't blame her. I don't want to see her bringing someone else pleasure."

"Remember that night in the club?" Luca asked, the

corner of his mouth upturned.

"What?"

"Sangre Dulce. We were working the Asgear case."

"Yeah, what of it?"

"You know I love Sam, so don't take this the wrong way. But that night on the dance floor…Sydney and I…when we danced. I know you watched."

"So?"

"So? You damn well know she was pleasuring me. Well, maybe she wasn't doing it entirely on purpose, but still. Dancing like that. And then you joined us for a little sandwich action. I was harder than a fucking rock out there. You knew." He laughed. "Not only did you know, you liked it."

Kade shook his head, unwilling to admit it. Seeing his best friend and Sydney enjoy each other had been a turn on, no doubt. But he'd always controlled the situation and he hadn't bonded to her yet.

"Don't tell me you didn't like it, because you did. And the three of us together, when I was injured? You both came to me in bed. Granted you knew I needed her blood, but still. When I bit her, she touched me. You would never have let it happen if there wasn't a small part of you that was open to it."

"It doesn't matter, Luca. Even if I did enjoy it, which I'm not saying, it was you. Sydney and I are both close to you. There's no one who fits that bill."

"What about Jake? He was with her when this demon shit all went down. Sydney knows him. He's wolf. His blood may help her transition more quickly."

"It's not happening," Kade said, but the idea lingered in his mind. While it was true that Jake had come to Sydney's aid, she didn't know him that well. As loath as he was to admit it, maybe he should ask the Alpha if Wynter was willing to help. Sydney and Wynter had cared for the child together, and since the attack, she'd come to visit her. His cell phone rang, breaking his contemplation. He slid his thumb across its glass and answered it.

"Kade," he responded.

"Detective Anthony Salucci."

"Anthony." Kade had expected he'd call sooner or later. Sydney's former partner still lived in Philadelphia. Prior to the accident, they'd kept in touch quite often. Lately, however, unless someone came to the house to visit her, she avoided speaking to anyone.

"What's going on down there? Syd isn't picking up my calls. I texted her and nothin'."

"Detective," Kade paused and glanced at Luca, "I'm very sorry to tell you..."

"What happened? No, don't tell me. She's not..."

"No...she's not dead," Kade replied, and took a deep breath. "There was an incident."

"Was she shot? Is she in the hospital?"

"No but...she was attacked."

"Goddammit, Kade. Why the hell didn't you call me? I would have come down there."

"There hasn't been time. And besides, she's recovering." Kade stalled and changed the subject. "I'm sorry but she isn't taking calls right now. I'd be happy to give her a message."

"Listen, I wanted to tell her first, but this concerns both of you now." He sighed. "There's been an escape."

"A what?"

"An escape. From prison."

"And you thought to call Sydney because?" Kade asked.

"The guy who escaped is dangerous. He's had a hard on for Syd ever since he laid eyes on her."

"You think he's coming down here?"

"*They're* coming for her."

"They're?" Kade's jaw tightened. As if she didn't have enough problems, some two bit criminal planned on attacking Sydney? He'd have laughed at the ridiculousness of the situation if it weren't for her seriously impaired state.

"Yeah, this guy. He's got connections. We busted him three years ago, and he's been tied to over twenty murders," Anthony told him.

"If he thinks he's coming to New Orleans to get Sydney, he's going to have to get through me first." Kade's eyes met Luca's.

"All the same to you, I'm flying down there. He's my responsibility and so is Sydney."

"She's not your partner anymore."

"She's my friend. You may be marryin' her but she'll always be my responsibility in my mind. I don't know what the hell happened to her and I can see you're not planning on tellin' me. Doesn't matter. I'll be there tomorrow and we'll work it out."

"You're welcome to stay with us, but you need to know something." Kade paused, concerned about how Sydney would react to seeing Anthony. "Listen, please don't take this personally, but Sydney may not be up for visitors. I think once she sees you, she'll be okay. But just in case she's not, I feel like I need to warn you."

"Then I'll visit with you. The best shot we've got to keep her safe is to work together. I want this guy and I plan on bringin' him back."

"Whoever even attempts to lay a hand on my mate will be going home in a coffin."

"I hear ya, but all the same, I'm coming to help."

"All right. We'll talk about it tomorrow." Kade clicked off his phone and slammed it onto his desk. "When it rains, it pours."

"I take it from your conversation the detective expects trouble. He worries too much." Luca took a sip of his drink and continued. "It's like you just told him; if anyone goes after Sydney, they won't be successful. They're mere humans. Criminals who've already been caught once. How bright can they be?"

"We should be cautious nonetheless. Sydney's condition is precarious at best." Kade picked up the bottle and poured another drink. "I'm worried about her. I know my girl. Something's cooking in that head of hers. She's going to strike out soon."

"Perhaps. It's to be expected, though. Even for a

mortal, she was a fighter. She's proven herself to be a fine asset."

"An asset, huh? You do have a way with words. How I missed your candor." Despite never being fond of humans, his friend had grown attached to Sydney.

"Miss Willows has always been stronger than most. Most humans are so very weak…a shame really."

"They serve a purpose. You and I both know it." Kade gave a small laugh, slightly amused with Luca's condescending attitude.

"So what to do with the human who is no longer human? You must learn to share donors. It can be quite pleasurable." A small smile crossed his face.

"She doesn't want a donor, that's the problem."

"Perhaps try a donor who'd agree to have you drain them artificially? They exist."

"No, it's a temporary fix. Not acceptable."

"But in the short term…"

"You and I both know she needs to learn how to feed on her own. I don't think it's the demon changing her. I've never heard of that happening. I tend to agree with Léopold. She's got some kind of block going on. I'll consider your idea about Wynter, though. I think knowing the person could make a difference. It's worth a try anyway."

"Did I hear the detective say he's coming for a visit?" Luca raised an eyebrow at him.

"Yeah." Kade stared into his glass, swirling the liquid and contemplating the bait his friend had laid on the table. Given the agony Sydney had caused her donors, he doubted she'd ever agree to feed from Anthony. He'd bet his life the detective would let her, however.

Sydney had confessed to him that, at one time, she'd considered dating Anthony, but never did so for fear of losing the respect of her peers. Kade had never been jealous of Sydney's friendship with her partner, because he knew with certainty that no one else was her mate.

As Kade downed the last of his drink, he heard the squeal of wheels in the driveway. His eyes met Luca's, anger flaring. As he'd suspected, she'd snapped; Sydney had left.

⤙⤙ *Chapter Three* ⤙⤙

Sydney had given it considerable thought. She couldn't go one more day depending on Kade for her survival. Her life had become miserable. There was no reasonable explanation for why she couldn't feed. If the demon had truly spawned her dilemma, then she was the only one who could regain control of the dismal situation. It had become a sickening ritual, watching Kade bite another woman, then dribbling the blood into her mouth as if she were a baby bird. A few tablespoons of blood hadn't been enough to fully heal her from the attack. She'd rather die than be forever reliant on the demeaning process that had barely kept her alive.

Sydney stood in front of the mirror gathering the courage to do what needed to be done. She finger combed her curly blonde hair, observing the dark circles that rounded her eyes. With shaky hands, she applied concealer to her pale skin. Tears wouldn't come, though her heart felt as if it had been shattered in a thousand pieces. She'd cried so hard in the past two hours that dehydration had set in, her mouth dried due to her stinted saliva.

Running her palm over the jagged scar on her abdomen, she closed her eyes. She resisted the temptation to stare at it one more time. The obsession to heal faster had done nothing but throw her further into a depression. Earlier in the week, she'd overheard Kade telling Luca that she should have been further along in her transformation. Her skin should have been flawless, yet everything about her was flawed.

Sydney reached for a t-shirt and tugged it over her head. She slipped into a prairie skirt, and stole a glance at the woman she didn't recognize. The tight fabric constricted her torso, showing her ribs. The weight loss only reminded her of how weak she was. She needed to drink more in order to recover.

Sydney rummaged through her purse, looking for her keys. As she did so, she was reminded that she no longer had a badge or gun. Her superiors had told her she'd been placed on sick leave but she knew it was just a matter of time before they fired her. Only humans worked on the police force. Supernaturals worked for P-CAP: Paranormal City Alternative Police, an organization she'd grown to tolerate but hadn't quite accepted. When she'd lived in Philadelphia, she and Anthony had worked with them on occasion on cases where human and supernatural crimes crossed paths.

As a police officer, she'd never gone out without a weapon. She thought it ironic that as a vampire she should be stronger than any human, yet she was the most vulnerable she'd ever been in her life. She closed her bag, resigned to the fact that she'd have to go without protection. At this point, it mattered little. The only thing she needed where she was going was cash. As she made her way to the car, sneaking by Kade, she knew what she had to do, and the only way she could do it was alone.

Sydney took a deep breath as she stepped onto the sidewalk. Gas lamps flickered overhead, their flames dancing to the bass that bled out into the street. The shuttered doors had been held back by brass hooks and eyes attached to the brick outer wall. Laughter spilled from a young couple exiting through the blue satin drapes that hung in the vestibule. A black wooden sign carved with gold calligraphy greeted patrons with a single word, *Embo.*

It wasn't as if Sydney hadn't been to clubs that catered to humans and supernaturals, places that allowed them to share blood and sex. Both Philadelphia and New Orleans hosted establishments that fostered the symbiotic relationship. But Embo was special. It was the only place she knew that had been restricted to vampires and humans only. No other supernaturals were allowed entrance. Of greater interest to Sydney was the purist nature of the feeding arrangements. Every human who stepped foot inside had unequivocally given their consent as a donor. And every vampire knew it. More importantly for Sydney, it was the only place in New Orleans where they provided the kind of food she sought.

Sydney grasped the curtain and pulled it aside. Her heart pounded against her ribs, the scent of incense in the air. A tall man dressed in a black suit fiddled with a reservation list, busily checking off names. She steeled her nerves as the maître d turned his attention to her.

"Good evening, detective," he said from behind a podium, not making a move to unchain the red velvet rope that stood in her way.

"No detective here. You see a badge?" Sydney opened her arms wide.

"Really, Miss Willows, then please tell me why you're here," he asked, a snobbish tone to his voice.

"The same reason everyone else comes here." Sydney resisted the urge to punch the arrogant ass as he rolled his eyes.

"This is no place for someone like you. Unless you have official police business, I suggest you return to your car. I'd be happy to have someone escort you."

"I just want a drink. Nothing more, nothing less."

"No offense, but I'm aware you're bonded to Mister Issacson. All of New Orleans is aware, as a matter of fact. There's no way your fiancé would allow you to come here by yourself. Besides, all humans who come to our club are donors. You and I both know that you cannot be a donor to another vampire. Anyone who looks at you is as good as dead."

"Do you want me to call him? I'm sure he'd love to

know who denied me entrance." As she spoke, she deliberately took slow breaths. Her mind swirled in chaos, but he'd never be privy to the conflict inside.

"I don't think that…"

"Sir, take a look at me," Sydney demanded. She didn't have time to mince words. Despite her efforts to avoid Kade, she knew when she'd taken the car, he'd hear her leave. She suspected he'd activate the stolen vehicle tracking and quickly learn of her location. "I said, 'look at me.' Do I look well? Better yet, do I smell human to you? I know you can smell me…just do it."

Sydney rooted her feet into the ground as he leaned toward her, coming within inches of her face. She fisted her hands tightly, readying to strike if he came any closer. Her nails dug into her skin, reminding her that even though she was now immortal, she could still very much feel pain.

"Vampire," he whispered, reaching for the brass clip on the end of the rope. "I'm very sorry, Miss Willows. I was not aware Mister Issacson had turned you. Please forgive me."

"Forgiven," was all Sydney could manage as a rush of breath hissed from her lips.

"Perhaps I should call your fiancé. This really is no place for a lady."

"As you so eloquently pointed out earlier, I'm a cop…was a cop. I think I can handle it." Sydney's eyes fell to the barrier and then met his. She wouldn't be intimidated from entering, dissuaded from her task.

"As you wish," he replied, ushering her into the foyer. "If I can get you anything at all, please let me know."

"Thank you but I'll be fine," she insisted.

Sydney never looked back as she moved toward her destination. The small foyer led to an arched hallway. Pinpricks of light poured from the unusual lighting fixtures, making it look as if the ceiling were made from stars. She pushed through a waterfall of bamboo beads, finally arriving in the main room of the club.

A fusion of Caribbean and new age décor surrounded her as she made her way toward the bar. Palm tree leaves appeared to sway, reflecting the soft flicker of tea lights. Traditional jazz music filtered throughout the airy space; a live band played in the far corner while patrons danced. In her peripheral vision, she caught sight of a tall brunette pinning a muscular man against the cream-colored wall. His torn shirt lay on the floor, a stream of bright red blood trailed down the side of his abs while he shook in a delirious state of bliss.

Sydney approached the bartender. He slid bottles of beer toward a group of twenty-somethings who nervously played with their hair extensions and chatted incessantly. Observing their behavior, she suspected it was their first time donating. A month ago, Sydney would have intervened, possibly used her police authority to escort them out of the club. Tonight, she felt nothing for the neophyte humans who sought the thrill of vampires. They'd committed, now they'd have to learn to deal with the consequences of their decisions. Whether they embraced or despised the experience, it was of no concern to Sydney. Like a speck of sand, they were insignificant in the grand scheme of things. People lived. People died. And some, like the immortal predators in the room, simply survived.

Sydney eyed the crimson tubes connected to large oak vats, disappointed that she simply couldn't drink it like water from a spigot. While the imported, aged blood was a delicacy, it wouldn't suffice to provide the nutritional needs of a vampire, especially a newly-turned one such as herself.

She caught the eyes of the attractive barkeep, who smiled at her. Shirtless, his loose white linen cargo pants hung precariously low on his hips. A flimsy drawstring, tied casually, swayed as he worked. Sydney noted there wasn't an ounce of fat on his artificially tanned chest. As he drew closer, she forced the corners of her lips into a friendly grin, and readied herself for the conversation that led her one step closer to her goal.

"Hello there, blondie. What can I getcha tonight?" His grey eyes twinkled as he spoke, and Sydney resisted the urge to ask him if he was vampire. "Drink? Donor? Sex? All of the above?"

"Donor only. No contact." Sydney wasn't sure what they called it; she only knew what she'd seen when she'd been in the club months ago. Working a case, they'd searched the bar for a suspect. That was when she'd discovered the special draining rooms, one for donors who sold their blood, but refused to be bitten. At the time, it struck her as perhaps a fetish. Clinical as it was, apparently the desire to drink from a glass appealed to some in their community. Likewise, squeamish humans who sought monetary compensation for their bodily fluids, had found a niche in the underground ecosystem.

"No contact, huh? You must be referring to our siphon specialty. It's extra, you know?"

"Cost isn't an issue." Sydney retrieved the cash from her wallet and slid ten one hundred dollar bills across the bar. She glanced over her shoulder, making sure she hadn't been followed.

"It's five hundred. This is too much." He counted out the bills and offered her back the extra money.

"Keep it for my tab," she told him. "How long will it be? I, um, I'm kind of in a rush."

"We usually have a wait, but," he picked up his iPad and began pecking at a scheduling app, "we can squeeze you in with number eleven. She just got in. Hold a second."

Sydney struggled to conceal the relief that overcame her. It wasn't ideal by any stretch of the imagination, but siphoning could be her salvation. As she waited for him to finish the arrangements, she scented the tinge of the iron delicacy in the air. *Hungry, so hungry.* Her hands shook and she steadied them onto her purse.

"This is Elia." He pointed to a petite woman who hurriedly strode across the dance floor. Her crushed black velvet dress reflected specks of silver under the black lights. "She'll escort you to your donor."

"Thank you," Sydney replied.

"No problem. Hey, listen, my name's Gil. If you're looking for some fun afterward, I'll be here for a few more hours." He winked.

"Um, thanks but I don't think…" She didn't bother finishing as she gave him a small wave.

Her guide gave her a nod and gestured toward the back of the room. Without speaking a word, Sydney obediently followed her. They weaved their way through the crowd of dancers, and her stomach clenched in anxiety and starvation. As they pushed through a set of swinging Cypress doors, the din of the club ceased. The calm-inducing spa-like atmosphere was a stark contrast to the actions transpiring behind the walls. As they made their way down the quiet hallway, she noted the sequentially numbered rooms. Elia abruptly stopped at eleven, and with a gentle knock, opened the door.

"Hello," a perky woman greeted them from inside. Lying comfortably on a dark leather chaise, she rested a paperback on her lap.

"Um, hi," Sydney answered. She looked to Elia, who continued to ignore her. "I'm not sure where you'd like me."

"She won't speak to you."

"Excuse me, what?"

"Elia is our technician for today but not present."

"But she kind of is present….she's right there." Sydney glanced to the woman who had begun to arrange the sterile dressings and tubing.

"Is this your first time?"

"Yes, sorry."

"I'm Mya," she said, offering her hand.

"I'm Sydney." She shook the woman's warm hand and quickly released it. Feeling disoriented, a wave of dizziness threatened to topple her.

"Hey, you okay? Here, sit next to me." Mya pointed to a soft cushioned chair.

"Thank you." Sydney quickly sat, placing her bag on the ground. She found comfort that the donor appeared entirely content, but Sydney still felt out of place.

"Siphoning really isn't as bad as they make it sound." Mya glanced toward Elia and then back to Sydney. "This experience is for you. I merely provide your food. And Elia, she's not present as in she's deliberately silent and will leave immediately after your blood is prepared."

"Why?" A part of Sydney just wanted to feed, but curiosity got the better of her. The human part had to know why they'd pretend as if someone wasn't even in the room.

"Not all humans and vampires publicly feed or have sex. Many of the vampires who seek the siphon option prefer the privacy we offer. While the intimacy of the feeding is removed, we can artificially provide the one-on-one interaction. When a vampire feeds from a human, they go unassisted. Therefore, it is just you and I. Elia is merely an instrument to our interaction. Therefore, she isn't *present*. She's not allowed to speak, because this is our experience. Your experience."

"I see," Sydney said. Admittedly, she'd never asked Kade about the rooms she'd seen here or why vampires would need blood this way. All she'd ever known was the bond that had existed between them.

"I know siphoning is a novelty for some vampires, but I do have some regulars. I mean, not all vampires want or need to…you know, make humans feel. They just want to eat, plain and simple."

"You mean sex?"

"Well, yes." Mya fingered the single braid that brushed her waist then raised her gaze to meet Sydney's. "It's none of my business why clients come to me but I suspect it's the same reason why a human wouldn't want to seek pleasure from another person when they've already committed to someone else. Even single people don't always want sex. And what are vampires really?"

"What do you mean?"

"Deep down, somewhere inside, they are human. Okay, well, I've met a few who really are no longer in any way human. But most have a tiny part of them that remembers."

"Why do you do this?" *Human*, Sydney thought. It hadn't been that long since she'd been turned. She swore she'd never become a monster, forgetting who she'd been, but she knew the truth. Her response at the bar demonstrated that she'd already changed.

"I know what a bite can do to someone," she replied, shaking her head. "I mean, I know how it feels. The intense emotions…the incredible sex. I simply can't risk becoming attached to anyone. It happens all the time."

"With donors?"

"I'm not supposed to talk about it. But it happens. I don't mind donating my blood. The money's good. This works for me. When I fall for someone, supernatural or human, I want to know them first."

"I understand." Sydney remembered the first time she'd made love to Kade, allowing him to infect her with his intoxicating bite. But she'd been attracted to him long before that amazing night. She'd never doubted the honesty of her feelings.

"If you don't mind me asking, why are you here today?" Mya rolled up her sleeve, allowing Elia to prepare her skin. Although she was speaking to Sydney, she paid close attention as the alcohol was applied.

"I, um, I can't feed." As the needle pricked Mya's arm, Sydney involuntarily dropped her fangs. Tears brimmed in her eyes.

"Hey, no worries. It's all good."

Sydney shook her head and looked away.

"I'm not sure what's going on with you but really, you're going to be okay soon. Look...see...the blood is coming. You're just hungry. There's no need to be ashamed."

Sydney's eyes fell to the end of the tube where the blood flowed into a tall champagne glass. Mesmerized by the sight of the dripping sanguine fluid, her eyes darted to Mya who gave her a comforting smile. Within minutes, Elia clamped the flow and offered the drink to Sydney. As she reached for it, Sydney once again looked to Mya as if seeking her permission.

"Please, take it," she insisted.

Sydney brought it to her nose and sniffed. The ambrosial scent caused her to salivate. Her animalistic response couldn't be stifled. With no emotional tie to the source, she freely drank the warm delicious sustenance. Unlike the sexual pleasure she'd experienced tasting of Kade, she likened it to eating a batch of freshly baked cookies. Perhaps it didn't offer an earth-shattering orgasm, but it was entirely comforting and provided satisfaction that could only be obtained from food.

When she reached the bottom of the glass, her eyes flew open. Electrified by the nourishment, her body tingled from head to toe. She shoved the glass onto a counter, barely noticing that Elia had left the room. Yanking her shirt upward, she ran her fingers over her belly. The scar had disappeared. Energy spiraled throughout her cells, and a broad smile spread across her face.

"It's gone, tell me it's gone," she shouted at Mya who laughed in response.

"What's gone? I don't see anything."

"Thank you. Oh my God, you saved me." Sydney rushed to Mya, taking her in her arms. Her laugher turned to tears and back to laughter.

"It's okay, now," Mya told her.

"I'm sorry. I know you don't know but I couldn't eat and now this…you…everything has changed. I feel so…so great. No, wait," she released Mya and took out a mirror from her purse, inspecting her newly rejuvenated skin. Pink-tinged cheeks and bright eyes stared back at her. "I'm fine. I feel so good. So strong."

"Well of course, you're a vampire." Mya sat up and steadied herself onto her feet.

"I didn't ask for this," Sydney confessed. She offered Mya a glass of juice that had been prepared earlier by Elia.

"Not everyone does," Mya replied, her expression somber. "I'm no vampire expert, but it's my take that most don't. But hey, look at humans. No one asks for what we're given either. Life can suck. We do what we have to to survive. And you, my friend, are doing just that...surviving."

"It's going to be okay...for both of us." Sydney wasn't sure what had happened to Mya but whatever it was, she suspected it had been horrific. She'd recognized the trauma, having seen it on many a victim.

"Yes." Mya offered a small smile.

"I don't want to be too forward, but is it okay for me to see you again?"

"Yes. I'm new so I'm only here once a week or so, so make sure you schedule at the front desk." She paused. "Listen, I'm not supposed to do this. I seem to be breaking rules left and right today, but here..."

Mya took a pen out of her bag and scribbled a number onto a napkin. Carefully folding it, she handed it to Sydney.

"My cell number."

"Are you sure? I don't want to get you in trouble."

"If you were a dude, there'd be no way. Even some of the supposed ladies in here are pretty aggressive. So I don't usually do this." She sighed, as if contemplating her decision to share her personal information. "No one deserves whatever happened to you. I mean, you need to eat, right? If for some reason I can't get here, you can always go see one of the other siphon donors. Twenty-four seven, Embo is open. But if you need someone…"

"Thank you," Sydney replied softly.

As she went to hug Mya, she heard Kade's voice bellow through the walls. He'd found her.

Chapter Four

"I've gotta go," Sydney said, grabbing her purse.

"Are you in danger?" Mya asked.

"No, I'm fine. I'll see you next week. Thanks." Sydney opened and shut the door, not wanting Kade to see where she'd been.

She ran down the hallway, grateful that he hadn't found her yet. As Sydney flew through the doors, she caught sight of Kade coming into the bar. She settled her back against a wall, and tried to gather her thoughts, so she could articulate the miracle of what had happened. In her peripheral vision, she caught sight of a familiar woman who approached from the dance floor. Sydney turned her attention to the human, studying her face, and soon realized that Kade had brought her to their house. At the time, she'd been in a daze, but memories of the buxom beauty flashed before her eyes; Kade trying to get Sydney to bite her. Unable to accept that she'd been turned, Sydney had refused. Her heart raced as she recalled the meeting. Unwilling to cause a scene, Sydney felt helpless to move as the donor cornered her.

"Can I help you?" The natural phrase of a police officer rolled off her tongue. She'd always trusted her instincts as a human, but as a vampire, all her senses were amplified exponentially. Confusion swept her mind.

"You know me, right?" the woman asked, her hands on her hips.

"You were at our home," Sydney responded. Her eyes darted to Kade who was deep in conversation with the bartender. He'd sensed her, she was sure of it.

"Yeah, that's right. I'm Gemma." She twirled a strand of her hair and gave Sydney a wide grin. "I didn't think you'd remember. You were kind of out of it."

"Yeah, I was sick."

"So, um, I don't mean to be so forward but you aren't married yet. And I noticed that Kade seems really unhappy. He used to be so…"

"My mate's feelings are none of your concern," Sydney said flatly. "Wait. What do you mean by 'he used to be'…used to be what?"

"Oh," she exclaimed innocently. "He didn't tell you? That's just like a man, isn't it? What I meant was that he used to feed from me. You know…before he met you. It's not the first time I've been to his house."

"What did you say?" Sydney felt her pulse race as her anger spiked.

"Before you met him, he fed from me. That's why he brought me to you. We know each other."

"He's a vampire. Of course he had to eat." Sydney's

eyes narrowed on the blonde's fingers as she toyed with the ribbons on her pink corset. Her tight black pencil skirt accentuated her ample curves. It was at that moment Sydney wondered how far Kade had gone with the human who clearly sought to provoke her.

"We kind of had a thing. I just thought with you being turned and all…I wasn't sure if you and he were still seeing each other." Gemma shifted on her feet and glanced over to Kade. She cupped her breasts, as if she were serving them up on a plate. "The last time I was at his house…"

"Our house." The rage within Sydney bubbled to the surface. This woman was an enemy, threatening her relationship with Kade. When she'd been human, she might have restrained her response. But now, her primal instinct was to protect, kill if necessary.

"I'm just sayin', it's not like you can feed him anymore. From what I heard, you can barely feed yourself." She laughed. "Honestly, if you can't take care of yourself, you should let him go. I really think you should…"

How does this insignificant twit know that I can't eat? Did Kade tell her? Does he really only want to be with a human, someone who can cater to all his needs? Doubt swirled within Sydney and as if a switch had flicked inside her, she lost control. Seizing Gemma by the neck, she slammed her face first into the wall. Instead of releasing her, Sydney held her tightly in place, coming up behind her. With her breasts tight against the woman's back, she yanked the hair out of the way, exposing the tight cords of her neck.

"Don't fucking move, bitch," Sydney hissed. Her fangs descended, rage filtering throughout her mind.

"I didn't mean to…" Gemma began.

"Shut the fuck up. You want me to feed, huh?"

"But he's not your…"

"Tell you what; you can have him when you pry him out of my cold dead hands." Sydney, poised to strike, caught Kade's gaze as she continued. "And about that feeding. How about I take you for a test drive?"

As Kade's hands landed on her shoulders, Sydney sank her fangs into Gemma's shoulder, slicing through her muscles. Before she had a chance to suck her blood, Kade extracted her off the human.

"No," Sydney yelled, aware that Gemma had fallen to the floor. "She's mine."

"Let her go, Sydney," Kade commanded. "It's alright. She's nothing."

"Leave me alone." Wild with anger, she flailed, attempting to free herself. The desire to kill consumed her.

"Okay, guess we're going to do this the hard way," Kade quipped as he slipped in front of her and hoisted her over his shoulder.

"Put me down! What the hell do you think you're doing?" Sydney clawed at his suit, barely cognizant of Kade climbing the stairs. *How many donors has he fucked? Brought to his house?*

"Almost there," Kade told her as they reached the landing.

"Just stop, Kade. Put me down," she pleaded.

Removed from the situation, the reality of what she'd done hit her. Sydney had never been one to take shit but she'd always kept calm, made decisions based on facts. Since she'd been turned, her every action tied itself to an emotion, rational or not. She sucked a breath, aware that she'd just bitten someone, intending to inflict suffering. If she'd been truthful with herself, she would have admitted that she'd flirted with the idea of killing the human. And she knew that she'd have done it without remorse.

As her feet hit the floor, she took in her surroundings. Kade had brought them up to a private terrace, which overlooked the club.

"Out," Kade yelled at two young women who were staring at them from a corner settee. Without argument, they scurried down the steps.

"You have no right to come in here and treat me like that." Sydney pushed the hair out of her eyes, scanning the balcony to make sure that they were alone.

"Wrong. I have every right to keep you from killing someone. You were out of control," he countered.

"Damn right I was out of control. That woman…that donor…you brought her to our house," she choked. Pacing, she raked her fingers through her curly locks. "I can't do this, Kade. You know I love you but I can't watch you with other women. You can't expect me to let you bring your lovers into our home."

"I'm not sleeping with her. I'd never do that to you."

"She told me you slept with her."

"I'd never lie to you," he asserted, deliberately lowering

the volume of his voice. "I may have been intimate with her, but it was long before we met. She's always been a reliable donor and that's why I had her come to the house. I haven't touched her since we met. I swear it."

"But you did touch her…a few weeks ago…after you turned me…"

"That day, I brought her for you only. I'm only going to say it one more time. I did not touch her," he insisted.

"Why would you ever bring her to our house?"

"I just told you why. I used her in the past. I know it was wrong but you have to put yourself in my position. I was upset and had to do something. Jesus, you almost died. I needed someone reliable to help. I don't like to just grab people off the street." Kade sighed.

"How many donors have you fucked?" Sydney put her face in her hands and blew out a breath. She lifted her gaze to meet his.

"That's not fair. We both have pasts." Kade paused. "Sydney, I'm really sorry. I know I shouldn't have brought her, but I was desperate to help you. I made a mistake."

"I can't do this."

"It doesn't have to be this way. If we can find a way for you to feed from a human, we can enjoy this together. Any woman or man is nothing more than food."

"But I can't, can I? Look at what's happened to me. I didn't ask for this."

"I am looking at you," he said softly. He approached her slowly and cupped her face, tracing his thumb over her bottom lip. "You're as beautiful as the day we first met. I can see that you ate. Tell me what happened. Please tell me you didn't kill anyone."

"I knew about this place…I'd been here on a case," Sydney stammered. She shouldn't feel guilty for coming here alone, yet shame overwhelmed her. Closing her eyes, she took a deep breath and then raised her gaze to meet Kade's. "I went to a siphon room. I'm sorry but I just had to do this. And it worked…I feel…"

"I can see you feel good again. But I don't understand why you ran. You have a bad habit of doing that, you know? No more running, Syd. Jesus. Come here," Kade ordered. He embraced his fiancée, a comforting hand massaged the nape of her neck. "We're going to figure this out. But you have to trust me."

"This is my fault. I did this." Within his arms, she relaxed. Confused, she held no answers. "Something's wrong with me. I can't ask you to give up the way you've lived for over two hundred years just for me. It's not fair to you."

"This isn't about fair, love. This is about us. You're the only woman in the world for me."

"But those women…"

"Shh." He kissed her hair. "They're nothing. There's never been anyone but you."

"I love you so much. I want this to work. Please." Sydney wasn't sure what she was even asking. With her life in a blur, she couldn't remember the last time they'd made love, that she'd felt like a woman, desired.

She glided her palms up his chest as he backed her

against the wrought iron railing. She wiped the back of her hand across her cheeks. Crying had never been her style, but her emotions spun wild.

"This will work. There is nothing that can ever come between us. Not this," his fangs descended, his lips pressed to her neck, "not this." Dragging his thumb across her lips, he teased them open. He ran his fingers over Sydney's teeth, and her own incisors dropped in response. "Your blood will be the only blood I ever want. Your lips…you, love."

As his mouth descended on hers, Sydney's heart raced. Allowing him to take control, she surrendered to his will. The taste of her mate spiked her arousal, and she was reminded how Kade could erase all worries from her mind. Coming alive with fire, she desperately kissed him in return. When he tore his lips from hers, she protested with a whimper.

"Turn around," Kade demanded, placing her palms onto the cool metal. He wrapped his arm around her waist. "These people…the vampires, the donors, they know nothing of our lives. Anyone who says otherwise is a liar."

"Kade," she breathed. Her bottom brushed against his rock hard erection.

"Nothing else matters. But you," he growled. He gathered up her skirt until he found the front of her thigh.

"Please, I…I missed you so much." Her line of vision drifted to the floor where onlookers had stopped to watch from below.

"From the moment we met, I knew you were mine. Nothing about your transition has changed that." Kade concealed his hand underneath the fabric, working his fingers into her panties. Cupping between her legs, he whispered in her ear. "Your pussy yearns for me, doesn't it, Sydney? Your master has been gone too long."

"I…I…" At a loss for words, she resisted the urge to run. The heat between her legs intensified, confirming what she'd always known. She belonged to him…her heart, her mind, her body. Despite her independence and bravado, the comfort of being cared for, loved, superseded any notion that she could survive as an island.

"I know what it's like to be so consumed with someone that you can't breathe without them. I may not have been the one starving this past month, but I've struggled to survive without you." He bit down on her earlobe as he slid a finger into her slick folds. Teasing her clitoris, he refused to give her a chance to retreat. "Goddess, I fucking missed you."

"Kade …they can see us," she breathed.

"That's exactly the point, love. I want them to see us. To see the pleasure I bring you." He plunged deep inside her pussy, withdrew and added two more. "Fuck, yes. You're so wet for me."

"I can't do this here…oh shit," she cried. It had been so long since he'd touched her. The ripples of excitement speared through her and she fought the orgasm she knew would come all too soon.

"Never again will you hide from me. Everything we do

we do together. Feeding. Fucking. All of it. Do you understand me?" When she didn't respond, he removed his hand and lightly smacked her mound.

"No, don't stop." He was angry that she'd fed on her own. She'd known what his reaction would be but had convinced herself he'd understand. Yet here he stood, teaching his lesson in front of an audience. She was helpless to argue as the ache between her legs grew.

"No running. Ever. Tell me you understand." His palm, that had rested on her belly, glided up her chest until he held her throat in his hands. Taking her chin, he turned her head so that his lips brushed hers. "Say it, Sydney."

"Kade," she breathed.

"Say it."

"I'm sorry…I knew. I needed to do this on my own. But I won't ever share you. I love you too damn much." She grasped his thigh, digging her nails into his leg.

"This pleasure, my soon-to-be wife," Kade pumped his fingers back into her wet core, "will only ever be yours."

"Ah, yes. Harder," she cried. Her head lolled back on his shoulder and she clutched his leg.

"And your blood…this pleasure is only ever for you," he said, his fangs slicing into her neck.

The familiar delicious sting of his teeth at her flesh sent her into a state of ecstasy. His bite was a validation of her role within his life. *Desired. Accepted. Loved.* She shook, the climax rolling through her. As his tongue laved over the wounds, she twisted around in his arms.

"Let's go home, love. I think we've made our point," he laughed.

"I'm not so sure about that. You started something, and I think we oughta finish it." No longer encumbered with concern that the humans doubted his commitment to her, Sydney pressed her palms to his chest, guiding him against the wall.

Kade thanked the goddess that he'd found Sydney when he had. He was aware that she knew he'd be able to track her. She'd been in the club long enough on her own that she could have gotten in serious trouble. Glowing, Sydney had been nourished. Even as she kicked and fought him on the way up the steps, he marveled at her strength. His happiness was countered with guilt for not suggesting siphoning from the minute she'd been turned. He knew damn well the method existed, that certain vampires preferred the complete lack of interaction it provided. But it was a course of last resort. Old school norms led him to teach her otherwise. She'd be extraordinarily vulnerable if she didn't learn how to obtain food on her own, to bite without pain.

Although Kade was relieved that Sydney had finally fed, Gemma was a complication he hadn't expected. At one time, she'd been a trusted food source. Irresponsibly, he'd fucked her on one occasion, but it'd meant nothing…to him. She'd played it down when he'd asked her to help with Sydney. He should have known that Gemma still had feelings for him. Bringing her home had been a lapse in judgment, one that could have cost him dearly. In Sydney's feral state, she surely would have killed Gemma.

Claiming his mate publicly had been the only way to convince her and everyone else at the club that she, despite being vampire, belonged to him. The rasp of his zipper coming down drew his attention back to Sydney, who clearly sought to continue the demonstration.

"What are you doing, baby?" Kade asked with a smile. He laughed as she pushed him over to the wall.

"What do you think I'm doing?" She lifted her shirt and cupped her breasts. Teasing her nipples into fine points, she licked her lips. The fabric fell and she grinned, slipping her hand into his trousers.

"You sure about this, love? It's not something you usually do in public…aw, fuck," he cried, as she took his dick in her hands.

"Yep…pretty sure," she responded with a giggle. Stroking the glistening come off the tip of his crown, she pumped him in her hand. "I want you now. No waiting."

"Not out here." Kade spied a door in the corner of the alcove. A storage closet, he hoped. Without bothering to remove her grip, he guided her toward it. They shuffled toward their destination, kissing as they went. Reaching for the door handle, he opened it and they laughed, realizing how desperate they were. She'd been ill for over a month. Like a shaken bottle of soda, they both were ready to explode.

"In here," Kade ordered. With his pants wide open, he dragged her into the small space and slammed the door shut behind them.

"Off," Sydney growled, dropping to her knees.

"Jesus Christ, woman…" His head fell backward onto a shelf, and he cursed as she tore down his boxers, unleashing his erection into her hands. She took his cock between her lips, and the momentary pain was soon replaced by ecstasy. He'd forgotten how amazing her hot mouth was, her talented tongue darting over the seam on his head.

"This cock belongs to me, do you hear me, Kade?" She gave him a wicked smile.

"Goddess, don't stop." He caught the gleam of desire in her eyes flickering red in the darkness.

"My cock." Laving upward with her tongue, she bit down gently as if putting him in a vise. "Every last inch of it."

"Fuck yeah," he agreed. Wrapping his hands into her hair, he guided himself through her lips.

Sydney stabbed her fingernails into his ass as he fucked her mouth. Kade's orgasm rose to the surface and he tilted her head backward, her face wet with saliva.

"Come here," he demanded.

Complying, Sydney shoved herself to her feet. She kicked off her shoes, and shimmied out of her panties. He slid his hands under her skirt, cupping her ass, and heaved her upward. She wrapped her ankles around his waist, her legs scraping the wall.

"Fuck me," she cried, dragging her incisors along his neck.

"Demanding lil' thing, aren't you?" He spun around, kicking a bucket in the process. Laughing, he reached for his shaft, still holding her to him.

"I need this. Need you in me...now. I don't care who hears."

"You better hold on, Syd. This is gonna be a rough ride." Kade readied his cock, lubricating himself in her wetness. He grunted as he buried himself in her.

"Holy shit. Oh my God," she breathed.

"Fuck, your pussy is so tight." He withdrew and slammed into her again. He felt a metal object digging into the back of his skull but pleasure outweighed the pain. He momentarily lost his concentration, and his grip slipped. "The shelves."

"The what?" Sydney asked, her hands wrapped around his neck.

"Brace yourself," he warned. His lips captured hers, his tongue invading her warm mouth.

Kade heard the ping of items scatter all over the floor as Sydney wildly reached for the shelf behind him. A mop fell over, barely missing his head. He'd have laughed had she not constricted around his cock, driving him to near climax. He felt as if he was a virgin again, unable to hold back.

"Harder," she cried into their kiss, desperation in her

voice. She clutched at the ledge, clawing her nails into the wood. "So close. That's it."

"I want to hear it."

"What?" She bit at his lips, locked in his gaze.

"I want this entire fucking place to hear you come." He thrust into her hard, causing her teeth to scrape his lips.

"Oh God, yes. Just a little more...oh shit." Sydney sucked at his lip, lapping the blood of her mate into her mouth.

"Can't hold it....Sydney...fuck, yes," Kade grunted. His balls drew tight, the pressure exploding inside him. Her pussy fisted him in rhythmic pulses, taking him from pure pleasure to unbridled release. His fangs descended, plunging into the soft flesh of her neck. Resisting the urge to take deep gulps of her essence, he controlled the impulse, gently suckling her skin and laving it with his tongue.

"I'm sorry. I'm so sorry." Tears flowed as she convulsed with him, her orgasm rolling through her.

"You didn't deserve what happened to you that day. None of this is your fault."

"I should never have left Logan's house. The demon...I knew there was something wrong. I fucked up."

"No, no, no. It's going to be all right. I promise you." He pressed his lips to her neck, her cheek, her hair, cradling his mate.

"Don't lie to me. Please. I couldn't take it."

"I have a plan. I always have a plan, my sweet Syd."

"God, I love you."

"I love you too. I swear to you on my life we will fix this." As Kade gently removed himself from inside her, he held her against him in the darkness, unable to let go.

~☙ *Chapter Five* ❧~

Kade lay watching Sydney sleep. It had been the first night in over a month they'd slept together all night in the same bed. While he'd never left her side after her attack, she'd been unconscious for weeks. After she awoke, she'd spent most nights pacing or crying, with no semblance of peace.

His conversation with Luca weighed heavily on his mind. As happy as he was that Sydney was temporarily sated, it was just a matter of time before she needed to feed again. She'd told him of Mya, and her desire to keep using her. But his concern remained that she'd never be fully independent.

Making love to her several times throughout the night, it wasn't lost on him that she'd never bit him. Her desire to had been palpable but he knew she resisted, afraid she'd hurt him, too. They couldn't go on forever like this.

His thoughts drifted to Anthony's impending arrival. Within hours he'd be at the house, and Kade still hadn't told Sydney about the prison break. With everything she'd been through, he didn't want to worry her. But the discussion was inevitable. As soon as she found out what had happened, he knew she'd want to help Anthony with the investigation. He'd argue that she was vulnerable, and she'd counter that she'd been healed, and was ready to go back to work. It would be nearly impossible to stop her.

But that was why he'd fallen in love with her. She'd always been strong, a protector of humanity. Given her challenging recovery, he feared she wasn't ready. Unable to feed properly, she'd soon become a danger to others if she was unable to control her impulses. She'd have killed Gemma if he hadn't stopped her. He anticipated she'd need several months to adjust to her transition. Having the discipline to restrain the urge to retaliate when faced with confrontation was a skill she'd hone under his wing. Letting her loose on the streets with her former partner could lead to disastrous consequences.

His primary concern kept circling back to her ability to feed on demand, especially if she became injured; something she'd be hard pressed to do if she was relying on a donor to surgically drain the blood from their vein. If what Léopold had suspected was true, that she'd developed a psychological block, they had to break the cycle. Kade reasoned that inducing pleasure during feeding would build her confidence and allow her to live a normal life as a vampire. He considered Luca's suggestion that Anthony could be the one to help. Only once had he shared Sydney and they'd both done it to save Luca from dying.

Kade leaned over, and pressed his lips to her cheek. She stirred for only a moment before continuing her healing slumber. He slipped out of the bed and went to the bathroom. As he stared at himself in the mirror, he contemplated the hard decision he'd have to make.

"Hello, Anthony," Kade said. The bitter pill he planned to swallow rested on his tongue. He wasn't sure how to broach the subject, but the idea was set in his mind. "You can put your bag over there."

"Hey man, how's it goin'?" Anthony replied. He shook Kade's hand and set his carry-on luggage next to the door. "Where's Syd?"

"Yeah, about that. She's still sleeping. Come into the kitchen and I'll get you some coffee." Kade gestured toward the hallway, talking as he went. "I really need to talk to you about what happened…she isn't herself."

"I need to see her," Anthony pressed.

"I've been thinking about this ever since you told me. When you tell her about the prison escape, you do know she's going to want to go after him? She's not feeling well, but that won't stop her. But she shouldn't. It's just not wise given her condition. How did this guy get out anyway?"

"How did he get out? Your guess is as good as mine. Can you believe they're still trying to figure out how the hell this happened?"

"Go ahead, have a seat." Kade turned on the coffee

machine, and rummaged through the cabinet for mugs. He pointed to a chair at the kitchen bar. "Tell me more about him."

"Thanks, it was a helluva flight. Someone behind me lost his cookies on the landing. I hate flyin'." Anthony rubbed his eyes and shook his head. "The name of the perp is Pat Scurlock. He's a real piece of work. We caught him holdin' a woman in a dungeon as a sex slave."

"What else?" Kade suspected there had to be more to the story.

"The vic we found in his house was alive. But the others..." Tony accepted a cup from Kade.

"Others?"

"Yeah, thirty-three others to be specific. They were dead. Found 'em all buried on his property."

"How exactly does something like that go unnoticed in the city?"

"He lived with his mother. We tracked him to a secondary location in the boonies. The property was under an alias name. Hundreds of acres with plenty of woods gives a serial killer a nice playground."

"So he goes it alone?"

"That's what we thought at first. But we found unknown secondary DNA on the bodies. Soon it was up to five."

"Accomplices?"

"Yes. His mother for one. She's behind bars. The rest have gone underground. All were into the occult in some form or another."

"What exactly were they into?"

"The women dealt mostly in psychic hotline sort of shit. They were busted a few times on shoplifting charges before all this went down with Scurlock. We're not likin' them for the actual killings, though. Most of the cases were brute strength; strangulation, beatings, things like that. More than a few had died of exsanguination. Two of them were decapitated. We're thinkin' they killed them and the women helped dispose of the bodies."

"If you caught this, uh, Pat, what about the other guy?"

"We got him on tape at a couple of local vampire clubs, but he's still out there, too. No offense, man, but you know that some of your, uh, vamp friends aren't exactly riding on the right side of the road. We've had some bad shit goin' on up in Philly, you know that?"

"Indeed," Kade agreed. Alexandra, a vicious vampire in Philadelphia, had a reputation for torture.

"I'm just sayin'. Things at home aren't as under control as they are down here. It's pretty ironic considering this is New Orleans, huh?" he laughed. "Anyhow, let's just say ole Patty has contacts in the supernatural community. We suspect he may have been involved in human trafficking."

"How's that?"

"Takin' victims, selling them to well-off vamps who need blood. There's been rumors of blood slaves, not kept individually, but in some kind of caged community."

"Jesus Christ, Anthony. Do they have evidence?" Long ago, it had been commonplace for vampires to capture and enslave humans. Sex, blood, it was stolen from the

LOST EMBRACE

innocents against their will. But in the past century, their community had evolved and it was no longer acceptable or legal.

"Honestly, we've got nothin' except the one victim we rescued from Pat's house. But she was delirious at the time and once she started her recovery, she clammed up. Blah, blah, blah, patient doctor confidentiality…not ready to talk…and now it's just a rumor."

"So why Sydney? Why does he want my fiancée?" Kade leaned against the granite countertop and crossed his arms.

"Because he's a fucking psycho. Because she was the one to take him down. My girl put a," Anthony paused at his words and corrected them, acknowledging Kade, "*our girl*…she plugged him in the shoulder, then handcuffed the fucker until the paramedics showed up. Testified against him."

"That would do it."

"He was kinda pissed. But then again they all are. The difference is that Patty started threatenin' her from jail. Phone calls at first. Once he lost those privileges, he managed to send her a few presents using connections."

"I'm afraid to ask."

"At first it was letters. When that didn't get a rise out of her, and you know Syd, it's gonna take a lot, our buddy sent her a tongue."

"What the…?"

"Yeah, a tongue. And it wasn't the kind you eat either." Anthony sighed and took a drink. "It was identified as belonging to a woman. It'd been preserved, pickled if you

51

can believe that shit. Never identified who it came from."

"When did this go down?"

"A few months before you met her. He was convicted about a year ago."

"So you're concerned he's got contacts down here? Supernaturals?" Kade stroked the scruff on his face, and mulled over what he'd been told. Despite Anthony's comments to the contrary, an evil undercurrent was alive and well in his city. His consistent and dominant rule was the only barrier between calm and chaos.

"Yeah, this guy has a real hard on for Syd." He coughed. "Uh, pardon my French. It's just he's gunnin' for her and we've gotta find him first. A good offense is the best defense with this guy."

"I'd better get Luca over here. We'll put some feelers out. If he shows up anywhere, he's as good as dead."

"Hey now, Kade. My virgin ears didn't hear that. Law enforcement, remember? As much as I wanna see some of these assholes take a dirt nap, I don't get to go around killin' humans, and neither do you."

"No worries, friend." Kade put his hand on the detective's shoulder and let the heat of Anthony's body seep into it. Even though Anthony wore a shirt, Kade could detect his pulse. Thoughts of blood twisted through his mind, and he imagined, but for a second, the intimate encounter they'd have should he agree to let them feed from him. Kade struggled to concentrate on the topic and crossed the room, staring out the window.

"You okay?" Anthony paused. "Ya wanna tell me

what's going on with Sydney? You never did tell me why she was sick….what happened?"

"There was an accident," Kade began. He reflected on the day he'd found her lying on the bloodstained pavement calling his name. "Anthony, I know you don't have a lot of experience with the supernatural. There was a time when Sydney didn't either." *No, I brought her into this world.*

"You'd be surprised what I know. Is she okay?"

"She was attacked…by a demon."

"What? Wait. Where were you?" Anthony stood, plowing his fingers through his thick dark hair.

"Before you even ask, yes, I fucking blame myself. But you know Sydney, and it wasn't as if she was alone. She was at Logan Reynaud's house. The Alpha of Acadian Wolves. It doesn't matter because what's done is done."

"What the hell's that supposed to mean?" Tony asked, his voice growing louder.

"She almost died…"

"But you said she's here, so what is it? Just tell me. Maybe I can help her."

"You can help her but I assure you it's not at all what you think." Kade faced Anthony, his jaw tight with angst. He flattened his hands on the cool stone counter and pinned his eyes on Anthony's. "I had to turn her. She's a vampire."

"No…no, this can't be happening…"

"It already happened. The transition…it didn't go well. She's not coping. She's having problems feeding."

"When did this go down?" he asked.

"About a month ago. You have to understand, she didn't want me to tell anyone." Although after last night's spectacle, the entire community would be aware of his fiancée's newfound state. "Well, more people probably know now but the point is that she wasn't doing well. She can't feed."

"Yeah, I just heard you say that, but what the hell is that supposed to mean? I don't know much about vamps but if she's still alive and obviously still tellin' people what to do, then she must be...you know...uh, drinking blood," Anthony choked out, shaking his head in disbelief.

"Keep your voice down," Kade instructed. He heard Sydney's footsteps in the hallway above him. "The drinking isn't the problem. She's having trouble biting."

"Is there something wrong with her teeth? I mean her fangs? Jesus, I can't even believe I just said that. How can she be a vampire? You should have found some other way to save her."

"Don't you think I would have? There was no other way." Kade slammed his fist down onto the granite.

"I'm sorry, it's just that Sydney...look, I know she loves you but it's not like she's exactly crazy about all this supernatural shit. She told me she didn't want to be turned, you know? This may be TMI, but we talked about a lot of things. She told me about your arrangement...you bite her, she drinks your blood and stays human. She never wanted to be anything other than what she was."

"I know. Believe me, I'm so fucking sorry...you have

no idea. And now she can't bite. Technically, she can, but she can't do it in a way that doesn't hurt the donor."

"Donor? Don't you mean human?"

"Same difference to Sydney. Our bite, it gives pleasure for a reason. It's an evolved survival strategy for our species."

"Nice," Anthony replied sarcastically.

"I won't apologize for our way."

"I'm sorry, man. It's just that this is all hard to take. I can't imagine what she's going through."

"Léopold thinks it's some kind of block. She loved it when I used to do it to her so it doesn't make sense."

"Exactly, Kade. She loves it when *you* do it, but not her. It's what she wanted when she was human, and now? Now, she's not, is she?"

"Just so you know, I've never heard of this happening," Kade continued. "Sure, some people are repulsed by blood at first, but once they feed, that moral concern disappears. Last night was the first time she fed successfully."

"I'm confused. I thought you just said…"

"She used a siphon donor. The blood is removed manually…drained into a glass."

Anthony grimaced, unable to conceal his disgust.

"It worked," Kade told him. "But unless she can do it the old-fashioned way, she'll be vulnerable, unable to feed herself should the need arise. Siphon donors aren't always available. Besides, when it comes to donors, most want the full experience, if you know what I mean."

"If most people are actually asking to be bitten, it must

feel pretty damn good," he laughed.

"Yeah, it doesn't suck," Kade joked. "Well, I guess it does but still, we make it as pleasant as possible."

"So, uh, what's the plan?" Anthony took a sip of his lukewarm coffee.

"I'll be frank. Until yesterday, there was no plan. I don't want to pressure you. What I'm about to propose…you asked how you can help." Kade paused, seeking the words that eluded him.

"Of course."

"It's just that Luca and I think that maybe if she fed from someone she knows…"

An amused smile crossed Anthony's face as soon as Kade spoke, but he remained silent.

"You're close to Sydney. If I wasn't totally secure in our relationship, I wouldn't suggest this, but…"

"You want me to let her bite me?"

"Yes, I do."

"I'll do it," Anthony responded without hesitation.

"You may want to take some time to make this decision."

"What's a little pin prick, huh?"

"I suppose you could say that." Kade smiled, pleased that he'd agreed quickly. But full disclosure was in order. "I think this may work, but you must understand. There are consequences."

"Like what?"

"First of all, this experiment could fail. The donors she's bitten…it wasn't pretty. In terms of pain level, it could feel like someone is pulling out your tooth." Kade raised an eyebrow at him. "Without Novocain."

"Hey, I'd take a bullet for that woman. I've been stabbed at least once. I think I can tough it out."

"Second, there's, uh, feelings. You know, like sexual ones. If we do this, it'll be intimate. We must make it as pleasurable as we can for her. Whatever she wants…whatever she needs." Kade could hardly believe he was agreeing to this, but desperation ran deep.

"Hold on now, are you saying that she," he pointed to the hallway, "and me," he placed his palm on his chest, "we'd be…together? No, no, no…you'd never…"

"It wouldn't just be the two of you." Kade laid it on the table, waiting for what he was proposing to take hold in Anthony's mind.

"You mean the three of us?" Wide-eyed, Anthony laughed as Kade nodded. "Well, shit…of all the things I thought were going to happen today, I did not expect to be propositioned by a vampire. For a ménage at that. Okay then."

"This isn't a trivial decision for me. Sydney trusts you. You're here. Most of all, you are willing. If this could work to trip whatever block she has, I know we'd both be grateful." Kade hoped he wouldn't change his mind. The more he talked with Anthony, the more certain he was that this would work.

"I'm in." Anthony stood up and nodded.

"You sure?"

"Yep, I'll do it."

"You need to know that Sydney...she doesn't know." Kade had heard Sydney's footsteps on the stairway and was hoping to finish before she reached the kitchen, but he'd run out of time.

"She doesn't know what?" Sydney asked. Spying Anthony in the corner, she squealed. "Tony! Oh my God. What are you doing here?"

She jumped into his arms and he spun her around. Kade smiled, observing the interaction. Maybe Anthony was exactly what she needed.

"How's my Philly girl? I missed you." Anthony hugged her, locking eyes with Kade. He kissed the top of her hair as if testing what Kade had told him.

"I missed you so much," she cried.

"Yeah, yeah, don't answer my calls. No texts. I think you forgot me," he goaded.

"Stop it." She pouted. Leaning back from his embrace, she slapped his arm. "I'd never forget you. Not ever."

"I don't know. I hear you've been kinda busy."

"He told you, didn't he?" Her face went flat, her eyes darting to Kade.

"Why don't you guys go into the family room and catch up," he suggested.

"Don't you think we should do this together?" Anthony asked, surprise in his eyes.

"I think old friends need privacy. You okay with that, love?" Kade crossed the room, settling a palm on each of their shoulders.

Sydney responded, reaching for him. He leaned down,

gently pressing his lips to hers. Uninhibited by Anthony's presence, they deepened the kiss. She swept her tongue between his lips. Passion stirred inside, and he lifted his lids to meet Anthony's gaze. He wanted him to have a small taste of what to expect. Regretfully, he did have business to attend to, and thought it important for Sydney and Anthony to have time alone.

Kade retreated, giving her, then Anthony a smile.

"Go talk with the detective. I'll join you in a bit."

"You invited him here?" she asked.

"Yes and no. He called me," he replied truthfully. "You weren't answering your phone."

"But you knew he was coming?" she pressed.

"I did, but this is much better as a surprise, don't you think?"

She eyed him suspiciously in silence and Kade knew she suspected something was awry. She'd know that Anthony would not visit without a reason, and Kade trusted him to tell her why he'd come to New Orleans.

"You heard him, Syd. Lead the way," Anthony interjected, his eyes meeting Kade's in understanding.

"I'm sorry, Tony. I didn't mean to be rude. This way," she said.

Kade watched with interest as she fell into her partner's trusted embrace and they traveled out of the kitchen. He prayed what they were about to do would cure her. But at the moment, more pressing issues required his attention. The human who planned Sydney harm was on the loose. Retrieving his phone, he texted Luca.

Chapter Six

Sydney's heart melted. For years, Tony had been her rock. Partners, they'd faced the best and worst of situations, surviving in the face of death itself. Next to Kade, he was the strongest man she'd known. *Loyal. Courageous.* Like coming home, she'd fallen into his arms. Emotion bubbled in her chest anticipating their conversation. He'd understood her desire to remain human more than anyone else.

"I'm sorry, I, um, I didn't return your texts." She moved to cross the room, but he held firm to her hand.

"No, Syd. Stay and talk. It's me," he pleaded.

"Tony, I can't...Kade told you everything?" Sydney turned her face away, unable to stomach the shame inside her. "I'm sorry, I should have been the one to tell you. I just couldn't do it."

"You should have told me, because you know what?" He reached to cup her cheek, forcing her to meet his gaze. "It doesn't matter what you are. You're my friend. My partner."

"Not anymore," she said, a sad reflection in her voice.

"Come here." Anthony led her to the couch. As they sat, he didn't release her. "Of all the people on God's green earth, I know you hate this. Remember when we first met that vamp you're marryin'?"

Sydney's eyes lightened and she gave him a small smile. She'd known he'd give her a pep talk. She considered that perhaps that was the reason she hadn't called him. She didn't want to feel good again. She deserved to suffer, given her mistake. She'd left the Alpha's compound, too confident she'd be able to protect them from the demon.

"You used to hate vampires. And maybe for good reason most of the time, but look at Kade. Luca. Even the wolves. You know I hang with Tristan now. He's one of the good guys."

"It's my fault. I thought I could handle it. Stupid. Stupid. Stupid." Sydney placed her palm on top of Tony's hands. She stared at her fingers, recounting what had happened. "I really don't remember that much. I went outside. This guy came at me. He looked suspicious but he was human at first. I fired my gun and then I was drifting away. I was alone."

"It's okay, Syd."

"Kade told me I was out of it for a few weeks. I couldn't even remember what they'd done to keep me alive." She sighed and gave Anthony a small smile. The light through the atrium doors flickered, and she took note how it deepened the color of his amber eyes. "When he told me what he did, I couldn't accept it. I was so angry at him for doing this. I should have died that day."

"He couldn't let you go."

"I know that, I really do. It's just at the time, I was so upset. And then the feeding…it's been a disaster. It wasn't the blood per se. I mean, you'd think I'd be disgusted drinking blood but I'm not. But hurting someone, that's not something I do to innocent people. The donor was screaming. It was awful. I just can't do that to someone. I *won't* do it."

"We're gonna work through this. There's nothin' we haven't faced. This is just one more thing. I promise you I'm going to be there for you," he assured her.

"There's nothing you can do. There's nothing anyone can do," she replied, her eyes brimming with tears. "I'm sorry I didn't call. I didn't want you to see me like this."

"This is exactly why I need to be here for you. Come here," he told her. Bringing her into his arms, he cradled her against his chest and stroked her hair.

"I missed you so much." Sydney laid her cheek against his soft cotton shirt and breathed in his masculine scent. Relief that he'd come flowed through her and she let herself revel in his comfort.

Anthony kissed Sydney's hair, refusing to let go. He couldn't believe what had become of her. Though he feigned a calm demeanor, his pulse raced in anger. How could this have happened? He wanted to blame Kade, but deep down, he knew that criminals walked the cities in all forms. The reality was that she could have been similarly injured on the force. Not everyone came out the end of a bullet the same way they were before they'd been shot. But it didn't matter; he'd made up his mind before she or Kade had a chance to ask. There was no way he'd leave New Orleans until she was healed.

His heart ached as she spoke, her words laced with despair. It didn't surprise him that she'd chosen not to tell him. His girl had pride as big as the city of brotherly love. All that she'd known had been destroyed, her life as she knew it gone.

Kade's request for assistance in helping her feed had been unexpected. Just the thought of Sydney at his neck caused his cock to twitch. He silently admonished himself for his response and tried to shake off the guilt. *I should be ashamed, for Chrissakes. What kind of a sick fuck gets off on his partner's problems?* He knew it was because he'd always been attracted to Sydney. They'd even kissed once, but she'd quickly shut down. She'd worked hard in the force and didn't want to jeopardize her reputation by dating him. He'd respected her choice and learned to accept their platonic relationship.

On the day she met Kade, he let go of the final piece of hope he hadn't known he'd possessed. At no point, however, had he felt bitter. He knew that being physically attracted to her and loving her as a friend didn't mean he was in love with her.

Sydney stirred in his arms and his thoughts moved to the escaped prisoner. He needed to tell her about Pat. No matter her own turmoil, she'd want to go after him. But in her vulnerable state, he thought she should stay within the safety of her home and allow Kade's security to protect her. Easier said than done, he knew.

"Sydney," he said, pulling out of their embrace. The aroma of her lily-scented hair teased his nostrils and he struggled to focus.

"Thank you for coming, Tony. Having you here…it just makes it a little better," she sniffled.

"I need to be honest with you. I came for another reason. I already told Kade and I probably should wait for him…"

"What is it?"

Anthony looked back toward the hallway for Kade.

"Just tell me already," she pressed.

"It's about Pat Scurlock." Tony hesitated, gauging Sydney's reaction.

"What? Please tell me that fucker's gotten a little poetic justice." Sydney wiped the back of her hands across her cheeks. Her shoulders straightened as she pushed away from Anthony.

"He's out." Like ripping off a bandaid, he thought it best just to do it quickly. He reached for Sydney's hand but wasn't fast enough as she jumped to her feet.

"What do you mean, he's out?" Sydney exclaimed. "How does a serial killer get out? Please tell me there wasn't some kind of legal loophole."

"Yes and no. He was granted a psych eval. His lawyer had him moved to a separate facility," he began. "They're still looking into it. Doesn't matter at this point, 'cause he's out. We're gonna protect you."

"Protect me?" She laughed. "No, no, no. It's the other way around. Somebody better protect him because this time he's not going back to prison," she promised. Holding up a palm, she silenced his attempt to interrupt. "This is the last straw. Just no."

"Maybe we should get Kade. We need to strategize what's gonna happen next. He says you're not feeling well."

"I'm fine," she insisted. "I'm not sitting at home while that psychopath comes after me. That's why you're here, isn't it, Tony? You and I both know what he's planning. He's coming after me. And he's got the contacts to do it."

"Okay, yeah. But Syd, I still think you oughta stay here and let Kade protect you. What I mean to say is that you look great." He stammered over his words. "Aw shit…it's just with you not being able to eat right."

"I've got options. I fed last night."

"Yeah, but Kade said that might not work in the long term."

"Goddammit, I'm so sick of this." She walked away from Anthony and stared out the atrium doors. With a heavy sigh, she continued. "Look, I know what I did isn't the perfect solution, but it worked. Besides, there isn't any other way. I'm stuck. I can't bite donors without hurting them."

"Maybe you just need a little help. I can help," he suggested, his hand on his chest.

"If you really could, I swear I'd let you, but so far, nothing has changed. I can't feed like Kade does. I have to just learn how to live like this. There is no other choice."

Anthony knew better than to argue with her. If Kade was right, she'd crash sooner or later. And when her world came crumbling apart, he planned on being there for her and Kade.

⤞ *Chapter Seven* ⤝

Kade estimated that Sydney would only make it through a few more hours before needing more blood. Unless a vampire was mated to a human, the reality was that one couldn't survive an immortal life relying on one donor. He knew Sydney had acquired Mya's contact information, convinced she'd forever feed from her. But siphoning was a temporary solution to a complex problem. A vampire couldn't function independently if they relied on others to prepare the blood.

Kade was certain he'd made the right decision by asking Anthony to help Sydney. He'd sensed Anthony's arousal as soon as he'd presented the idea. Her partner had happily agreed, confirming what Kade had always suspected; Anthony desired Sydney. Still unsure of how to broach the topic with Sydney, he considered that it might be best to wait until she showed signs of hunger. At that point, she might be more willing to accept his proposal.

One thing had become clear since his conversation with Anthony; locating and killing Pat Scurlock was a priority. While vampire activities were generally under his tight control, a small element of unrest always existed. Kade had contacted P-CAP, making them aware of the escape and potential supernatural involvement. When he'd spoken with Logan, the Alpha had assured him that his pack would alert him if they heard of any suspicious activity going down on the streets.

A knock at the door interrupted his thoughts. He shoved out of his chair, making his way toward the foyer. He opened the front door, and Luca's stern expression met his. Dominique, who'd become Luca's security assistant, followed. While she'd never intentionally hurt an innocent human, she'd proven herself deadly on many occasions. Kade shook his head when he caught sight of her skin-tight black catsuit and over-the-knee boots. Her red hair had been twisted up high on her head into a ponytail. If there ever had been a vampire who reveled in her race, it was her.

"Come in." Kade gestured for them to enter.

"You talk to Logan?" Luca began.

"Yes. They're going to keep a strong presence in the city," Kade replied.

"How is Sydney doing?" Dominique asked.

"She's doing better today." Kade hesitated. "She fed last night."

"Siphon donor." She sniffed with contempt. "It's weak."

"I'm with her on that one," Luca added.

"Yes, I know," Kade agreed. "But I've got a plan for

that. I've given some thought to what we discussed.

"You mean…a friend?"

"Anthony's here."

"The detective? From Philadelphia?" Dominique asked.

"Yeah. Her partner," Kade confirmed.

"So she's agreed?" Luca questioned with a cocked eyebrow.

"She doesn't know yet. We'll discuss it later."

"I think you might want to tell her sooner than later," Luca suggested.

"Can someone clue me in as to what you're talking about?" Dominique whined. "Why are we just standing here anyway? Let's get this show on the road. I'm looking forward to staking out that Matt guy."

"Pat," Kade corrected.

"Matt. Pat. Whatever," she sighed and flicked her nails. "So, where's Sydney?"

"Sydney's in the living room with the detective. We don't know where we're going, let alone who's going. I called you over to talk to Anthony and strategize."

It wasn't as if Kade hadn't given it thought. On the contrary, he knew exactly what he planned to do. If he had to visit every blood club in the damn city, he would. The last thing he needed was this asshole criminal stirring up trouble. All it took was one vampire with delusions of grandeur to cause an uprising. His cell buzzed and he swiped his thumb across the glass. He read the text, and blew out a breath.

"There's been an attack at Embo," he said.

"What happened?" Luca asked.

"I don't know. The text is from Gil Martin."

"The bartender?"

"Yeah. Looks like a couple of vampires are dead. P-CAP is on the scene."

"Well, shit."

"It's time to roll. I'm gonna go tell Anthony. Get the car," Kade ordered.

·❦· *Chapter Eight* ·❦·

Kade took in the scene at Embo. Blinding house lights illuminated the blood-sprayed walls. Bar stools and chairs strewn about the floor indicated signs of a struggle. From what he could tell, there weren't many witnesses alive to question. The only employee he recognized was Gil Martin, who stood behind the bar pouring himself a shot of tequila.

Despite his best efforts to convince Sydney to stay at home with Dominique, she'd insisted she'd be safer with him. It wasn't as if he hadn't expected her refusal, but he gave her points for persuasion. She and Anthony stayed close as they checked out the debris, never leaving his sight. He kicked through a pile of ash and assumed that a vampire had been staked. His gaze caught Gil's and the bartender nodded in silent understanding.

"Who did this?" Kade asked.

"There were four of them. All wearing masks."

"Ski masks?"

"No, man. I'm talkin' full head coverings. Devils and

animals."

"Okay," Kade breathed. "Well, this is New Orleans. They could have gotten them just about anywhere."

"Not sure if this matters, and you know I already told P-CAP, but the masks…they weren't the cheap ones. They were leather. The kind some of the more expensive stores sell."

"Or they could have bought them on the internet."

"Yeah, I don't know. It all went down fast. I would have called you sooner but you know how P-CAP is."

"What time did this happen?"

"It was about six or seven this morning." Gil slammed the liquor down his throat, coughed and scrubbed his hand over his hair. "I was getting ready to turn things over to the dayshift. Counting tips. Not many people are here at that time."

"Who was?"

"They killed Sean. You know, he works the front. The band had already gone. There were just a few other vamps still here. Both are dead. You're walkin' in 'em."

"Donors?"

"Yeah, they seemed more interested in them."

"What're you talking about?"

"They wanted names. Wanted to know who was here, like they were lookin' for someone. I gave them the inventory list."

"Where's the list?"

"I don't know. It's on an iPad. We keep track of everything that way. I gave it to one of them and that was the last I saw of it. Hey, when the bullets started flying, I lost interest."

"Syd, Anthony. We're looking for an iPad," Kade called out. "Let's get back to the donors. How many were still here?"

"I don't know. I think maybe six or seven. A few dove back here with me. P-CAP took them down to the station." Gil looked over to a pool of blood underneath one of the tables and wiped his hand across his mouth. "Two are dead. One they took out on a stretcher. Not sure if she'll make it."

"Anyone else?"

"Yeah, man." He paused, tightening his grip on the bottle. "Gemma."

"What about her?" Kade was surprised she'd stayed after Sydney's attack, but he also knew how much she got off on vampires.

"They took her. She was alive, though." He shook his head and put the rim of the bottle to his lips, not bothering to pour it in a glass this time. "She was screaming. It all happened so fast."

"How do you know it was Gemma if you were back here?"

"I've worked here a long time. You know she's a screamer." He blew out a breath. "Shit, I know that's wrong to say at a time like now, but it's true. I heard her scream, and peeked over the bar for all of about two seconds before a slug whizzed by my head. I saw them dragging her out of here. For the record, I did shoot back.

I keep a handgun back here but it was no match for what they were packin'. Fuck, this has been a night."

"So you think the perps were vamps?"

"Only one. The way he took out the others…he had to be a vampire. The other three seemed human."

"You sure?"

"I've been working here for five years, boss. I'm tellin' ya, I know the difference. Mask or no mask."

"This it?" Anthony interrupted. He held up a black leather case and opened it.

"Yeah," Gil responded. "We've got an app that tracks the appointments. It's what was up when I gave it to zebra guy."

"It's busted," Anthony said.

"Let me see." Kade took the iPad from Anthony, observing a web of cracks across its glass. He pressed a button and it flared with light. "Still working."

"Well, that's something."

"You keep personal information on employees?" Kade asked. His eyes darted to Sydney, whose shocked expression told him she already knew what he was about to say.

"Yeah, we've got personnel files but we keep addresses and phone numbers stored in there so we can call in staff when we need to…go pick them up if they need a ride. Stuff like that."

"They were looking for her." Kade flipped the tablet toward Sydney, so she could view it. Mya Everhart's address and appointment information flashed across the

"He went after her because of me," Sydney whispered. "Shit. How could he have known?"

"Someone told him," Kade said, his eyes meeting Gil's. After their performance on the balcony, it hadn't been a secret that both he and Sydney had been at the club.

"Hey, I don't know who you're talking about but whoever it is, ya'll know I wouldn't tell anyone anything. Look at the donor list if you're looking for a suspect. Humans don't all get the privacy rule. Just sayin'," Gil said.

"We've got to go to Mya." Sydney tugged on Kade's arm.

"I think we should get you home," Kade suggested.

"This is my fault. I came here. I used Mya. There's no way I'm not going to check on her."

"Look at me," Kade said, taking her hands in his. Her cheeks remained flush with color and she appeared healthy.

"I'm fine. I swear it."

"The second you feel the slightest twinge of hunger, we're going home. Understood?"

"Yes, I promise."

"Let's go," Kade reluctantly agreed.

As they left Embo, he pulled Luca aside and asked him to go ahead with Dominique to Mya's apartment and make sure it was clear. He caught Anthony's look of concern as the detective ushered Sydney into the car. Someone had alerted Pat that Sydney had been at Embo.

It was likely the informant was alive and well, assisting Pat, and looking to lure Sydney into a trap with Mya.

It wasn't as if Sydney hadn't been to a crime scene before, but this was personal. Mya was missing because of her. She studied the décor and took note of the perfectly straightened books that sat on a dusted bookshelf. A small trail of destruction led from the foyer into the bedroom, everything in its path strewn onto the floor. She spied an overturned picture frame on the carpet and bent over to retrieve it. Sydney ran her finger over the edge of the cold metal frame and picked away the broken glass. Underneath, Mya kissed a fluffy white lap dog, a pink diamond collar around its neck. Every detail about the apartment told a story of an innocent young woman, one who appeared to be in college. Her psychology book lay open on a small kitchen table, and Sydney wondered how the fresh-faced coed had found herself employment as a siphon donor.

Kade waved to her, gesturing to the bedroom. She entered, scenting the blood, but concealed her reaction to the scene. A torn shirt lay on the floor. A set of bra and panties were tied around one of the poles of the white four-poster bed. Dark brown bloodstains were splattered across the pink sheets.

"Are you sure you wanna stay?" Luca asked Sydney.

When she nodded, he leaned over and sniffed the linens. "There's semen. It's fresh. It's possible she was raped."

"It would be in line with Pat's M.O.," Anthony interjected.

"Yeah, it is." Sydney turned her head, sickened by the sight. She made her way into the tiny bathroom and what she saw took her breath away.

"Wait a minute, Syd," Luca said. "I didn't have a chance to tell you…"

"Kade." Sydney's heart caught in her chest as she saw the folded note taped to the mirror. Kade went to reach for it but she blocked his hand. "No, he left this for me."

Her hands shook as she tugged at the smooth paper, careful not to tear it. *Pat Scurlock. He attacked Mya because of me.* Carefully, she opened it, a gasp choking in her throat as she read it. *You took my girls. Now I'm taking yours.*

"He's not going to get to you," Kade assured her.

"He's going to kill her," Sydney whispered. Dizzy, she gripped the sink.

"Syd. You know him. He never kills right away," Anthony said

"No, he'll play with her, torture her. I don't get it, though. Who is the vampire helping him? What could Pat possibly have that he'd be worth causing this kind of trouble in New Orleans? Maybe he's not from here."

"It could be a 'she'," Luca commented.

"A woman?" Sydney asked with surprise.

"They had on masks. But who knows? It all went down

fast and Gil didn't see much from behind the bar."

"Gil never mentioned he scented or suspected it was a woman," she countered.

"It's unlikely but still possible," Luca continued.

"I guess."

"Back to your other question; why does a vampire involve himself with miscreants?" Luca took the note from Sydney's hands and studied it.

"Power would be the obvious answer, but if there was one strong enough to challenge me, why would he wait for the help of a human? It makes no sense," Kade said.

The conversation faded as Sydney spied the red spray on the flowered shower curtain. Bile rose in her stomach and she fought the pangs of hunger that arose out of nowhere. She closed her eyes briefly, and attempted to gather strength. Something was happening to her. The rush of Mya's blood waned. She'd need to feed, find another donor. Yet curiosity drove her as she put one foot in front of the other. Her fingers curled into the nylon fabric. As she pulled it across, a thick trail of caked blood clung to the textured fiberglass tub. A tunnel of black engulfed her vision as she pointed to her name, which was written across the white tiles.

Chapter Nine

Kade gently laid Sydney onto the crisp cotton sheets. After she'd fainted, he'd gathered her into his arms, cursing himself for not seeing the signs. He'd dismissed her shaky hands, but knew she'd never show fear. Before her accident, the threat in the shower wouldn't have caused her to falter. While she'd been temporarily nourished, it wasn't nearly enough for a new vampire to thrive. As if she was a newborn, she'd need frequent feedings.

When he'd left Mya's apartment, he'd instructed Luca to wait for Xavier, so they could turn it over for clues. Despite his orders, Kade suspected they wouldn't find anything else. Pat Scurlock meant to toy with Sydney. Like a cat batting around a mouse, he'd play with her first, making his kill all the more sweet. Delighting in a sick sense of torture, Pat sought to instill both fear and guilt.

Kade had asked Anthony to help him transfer Sydney back to the house. He played the scenario in his head, the act scrolling through his brain. A mixture of excitement and apprehension arrested his thoughts, and he prayed

Sydney would accept the inevitable.

After they'd arrived home, he'd given her a bath. Cleaning the stench of the evening away, he'd washed Mya's blood from her skin. He'd dressed her in a warm robe and brought the covers up over her hips. Brushing a stray hair from Sydney's eyes, he studied her face and considered how much he loved her. Sharing her with Anthony would be the ultimate act of devotion, yet he was fully prepared to see it through. He wasn't sure why he thought it would work, but instincts told him that she'd never allow herself to hurt her friend.

Kade turned his head toward the door, where Anthony stood silently watching. Wearing only a pair of pajama pants, he stood bare-chested. Kade gave him a small smile and waved him into the room. As the detective made his way toward the bed, Kade leaned to kiss Sydney's forehead. Her eyes flickered open in response. She stared up into his eyes wearing a look of confusion.

"Hey there, how're you feeling, love?"

"I, um…" Sydney's eyes darted from Kade to Anthony, who stood next to the bed. "How did I get here?"

"You had a little spell is all."

"I passed out, didn't I?" She groaned.

"Not unexpected, I'm afraid. I should have watched you more carefully," he apologized.

"This isn't your fault."

"I should have known you were about to get sick."

"How would you…?"

Kade cocked an eyebrow at her and smiled.

"Hmm…you know everything, huh?" Sydney moved to sit up, but fell back onto the pillow in exhaustion.

"Just relax, now."

"Back in the bathroom, I don't know what happened. I remember feeling dizzy, hungry. I need blood again, don't I?" she asked.

"I may omit details every now and then," he gave a small laugh, looked up to Anthony and back to her, "but I'll never lie to you. You need to eat."

"Where am I going to get blood? Mya's gone." She sighed and closed her eyes. "I can't do this, Kade. I can't bring one more donor into our house. I can't do it. There's something wrong with me. I'm a terrible vampire."

"No you're not. You're just a little fang challenged." He smiled down at her, gently sliding the back of his hand over her cheek.

"I'm the worst." Her gaze moved to Anthony, who leaned against the wall, his arms crossed. Her eyes lit up and she reached for him. "Tony. What are you doing all the way over there? Come here."

"You scared me, there. How's your head?" he asked.

"My head?" Sydney smoothed her hand over her hair. When she found the knot, she grimaced. "Shit. I thought being a vampire was supposed to give me some kind of super healing power?"

"You need to feed," Kade told her.

"But I did."

"More often. At least every day for a few weeks. It

won't always be this way, but you haven't been well."
Kade brushed his lips to her forehead.

"I can't believe he took Mya," she began. "If we hadn't
made a scene…we did this."

"Stop it, Syd." Anthony's eyes met Kade's. He moved
to sit on the bed, bringing his legs next to hers. He shoved
up onto his side, resting his head on his hand. Bringing
her hand to his chest, he continued. "You know Pat better
than anyone. The women he takes. The ones he tortures.
He's been after you for months. But not once did you
flinch. Not once did you cave to the phone calls or the
letters. And I'm not going to let you now. We," he glanced
to Kade, "aren't going to let you be a victim. If you were
feeling better, you'd kick both our asses."

"How am I supposed to fight like this?" she replied.

"I want to help you." Anthony kissed the back of her
hand, refusing to let her go. His eyes met Kade's.

"What do you mean, *help* me?"

"Anthony's going to be your donor," Kade said, his
voice calm and caring. He knew she'd protest at first but
he wouldn't take no for an answer.

"No." Sydney tried unsuccessfully to sit. She grunted
and fell backwards once again.

"Yes," Anthony insisted. "Listen, Kade's been talking
to Léopold about what's causing this to happen to you,
and I know you know this already, but he thinks you need
a friend to help you get through this thing. It's just like
anything else in life. You have an accident and you're
afraid to get in the car and drive. Fall off a horse and

you're supposed to get back on."

"I was never on the horse."

"Okay, bad analogy but the principle is the same. Until Kade, you'd steered clear of the supes. I know you love Kade and you've become friends with some of his friends, but for a long time, all you saw was the bad side of vampires."

"And humans," she added.

"All the donors we've had to date have been strangers. And normally that's fine," Kade explained. He'd thought discussing his proposal would be the easiest path to get her to acquiesce, but he was starting to rethink his strategy.

"I can't control it. It's not like I haven't tried," she told them, shaking her head.

"I know, but we need to try again…you'd never hurt Anthony. Please. Let him do this for you, Sydney. Let him do this for us. Once you learn how, you'll be free."

"I don't know. This seems wrong. What if I can't control the rest?"

The rest? The devil is, indeed, in the details. Kade knew what she was thinking. It was perfectly normal to arouse and be aroused when feeding, but the act itself could be restrained. One learned discipline through experience, but first she must learn the basics.

"I'll do that for you." Kade took her hand in his. Like mirrored souls, he and Anthony flanked her.

"I don't know…are you sure about this?" Her eyes darted from Kade to Anthony. "Tony, if this works…I need to know you'll be okay afterward. I don't want to use you."

"I'll be fine. It's not like it's a secret that I find you attractive. But we both know that we aren't meant to be together…not that way."

"You know I love you, Tony, but I'm *in love* with Kade." She gave him a small smile.

"I get it, Syd. It's okay. I want to do this for you."

"I don't know if this will work," she hedged.

"This will work, love. All you need to do is trust me." Kade pressed his lips to hers, indulging in the warmth of his mate.

"I don't know," she whispered into his kiss.

"Trust us to take care of you." Kade spoke into her mouth.

"Yes," she agreed softly. Her face flushed as she caught Anthony watching her.

Reluctantly, Kade broke away and slowly turned her to Anthony, who brought his palm to her cheek. "I want you to taste him…scent him. Know your prey."

Sydney's mind warred against what she yearned for, Anthony's vital essence flowing beneath his skin. As she took his wrist to her lips, she shivered with desire. An ache grew between her legs, arousal flowing through her veins. She fought the burn in her gums, concerned about the pain she'd cause Anthony. Her eyes flew open to Kade, who stroked his hand over her hair. Unsure, she shook her head in refusal, yet she never let go of Anthony's arm.

"What's wrong, love?"

"I…I don't want to hurt him." Sydney's eyes fell on Anthony, whose erection pressed into her hip.

"We'll do this together," Kade promised. He leaned forward and brushed his lips over her forehead. "All of us."

Her chest constricted with emotion as Kade's fingers trailed down her collarbone. She relaxed into his touch, his strong hand massaging her shoulder. Their eyes locked, and her anticipation heightened as she felt a tug on the belt of her robe. He opened the fabric and the cool air teased her nipples. Exposed, she arched her back as he thrummed the pad of his thumb over one of her taut tips. Moaning softly in arousal, her mouth grazed over Anthony's arm.

"That's it. Let go," Kade told her. His eyes caught Anthony's and he nodded.

"You sure?" Anthony hesitated.

"Tony," she began. In tandem with her arousal, the urge to bite him grew stronger. She took his hand and rested it on her bare stomach. "Please. I'm scared but I want this."

"Syd," Anthony breathed. He tore his arm from her grasp and slid it around the back of her neck.

As his lips met hers, she opened to him. His tongue swept into her mouth and she whimpered in pleasure. Unlike Kade's possessive kiss, his was soft and gentle. His succulent taste flared every nerve in her body, and she wrapped a leg around his waist. Allowing Kade to undress her, she breathed into Anthony's lips as her mate's bare chest grazed her back. Kade's strong hand cupped her breast, his cock prodding her bottom.

"This is what you need," she heard him tell her, his fangs scraping her shoulder.

"Kade, I…ah," she cried. Her eyes focused on Anthony's; his cheek brushed into her cleavage, his soft lips grazing over the swell of her breast. The unmistakable feel of Kade's fingers slipping into her wet folds left her pleading for more. "God, yes."

"That's right, feel me inside you. Let your senses take over. Scent Anthony's blood. Can you feel his pulse? Take what he offers. He wants you to have it."

"But what if I…"

"You won't hurt him. It's okay. He's agreed to this. You can do it. Give him the pleasure he seeks," Kade commanded.

Granted permission to enjoy the experience, Sydney smiled. She slid her hand into the front of Anthony's pajama pants and gripped his cock, swiping the glistening wetness over his slit. A rush of dominance surged through her as she heard his groan of pleasure. His head lolled back onto the pillow, exposing the cords of his neck as she lapped his skin.

"That's it, love," Kade encouraged.

Sydney's hips gyrated against the heel of Kade's hand, his fingers plunging deep inside her. His thumb grazed her clitoris and her breath caught. Drenched in arousal, the walls of her tight channel contracted as he fucked her. Anthony took her nipple between his lips and sucked hard. The seductive pain rolled through her and she cried out, her fangs distending. She fisted Anthony, rhythmically stroking his cock.

She growled as Kade lifted her hips toward him, his fingers still deep inside her pussy. He pushed her legs open with his knees and began to tease her opening with the crown of his dick. She protested as he withdrew his fingers and spread the wetness of her core through her folds. He applied pressure to her clit with his thumb, and Sydney responded, tilting her ass toward him.

"Fuck me," she pleaded. Her mouth dropped to Anthony's neck. The scent of his delicious blood called to her and she flicked her tongue at his shoulder. Her razor-sharp teeth scraped his skin, drawing a thin white line across his flesh.

"Ah yeah," Anthony grunted as she cupped his balls.

Jolted by the sound of Anthony's voice, Sydney froze.

"What's wrong?" He sighed, leaning his forehead onto her shoulder. "Why are you stopping?"

"I hurt you," she whispered, jarred from the moment.

"I'm fine. I want this. You won't hurt me...you'd never hurt me."

"Give me your arm," Kade told him.

Anthony gave him a look of confusion, but complied. He released Sydney's breast and reached his arm around the back of her neck within inches of Kade's lips.

"We'll do this together, love. You with me?" he asked,

his eyes meeting Anthony's.

"Fuck, yeah. Syd, ya got me hangin' by a thread here," Anthony moaned.

Fear had strangled Sydney for far too long. Releasing her anxieties, she bared her fangs, allowing herself the freedom to take what he offered. She nicked his lip, a drop of his blood coating her tongue. Wild with arousal, she grunted as Kade slammed his cock into her pussy.

"Yes, yes, oh God, I want you, Tony," she rambled as she fisted and stroked him hard.

"Faster," he ordered, thrusting his shaft into her palm.

"Now," Kade instructed.

The sight of his sharp teeth inches from Anthony's forearm drove her into frenzy. Lost in her desire, she followed Kade's lead as they both sank their fangs deep into Anthony's flesh. As he thrashed in pleasure, his sweet blood flowed freely down her throat. Her mind open, she focused on driving him into a state of unbridled euphoria.

"Holy fuck, yeah...I should have...this feels...don't stop," Anthony cried.

Blood ran down his neck and over her lips, and Sydney drank her fill, lapping her tongue at his wounds. Her own orgasm built as Kade plunged into her from behind, his fingers pinching her swollen nub.

"Harder," Anthony yelled.

Sydney caressed his sac while pumping him faster and faster. He screamed in climax, his seed spilling into her hands. As Kade released his arm, she removed her mouth from Anthony's neck.

"Get up," Kade demanded. "Hands and knees."

Sydney obeyed without argument. After Kade had shared her with Anthony, he'd dominate every square inch of her body. Out of the corner of her eye, she smiled as she spied Anthony lying on his back, still reeling from his orgasm. The glow on his face exuded satisfaction and his eyes caught hers right before she felt Kade thrust into her from behind. His fingers dug into her hips, and she concentrated on balancing herself. Eagerly awaiting his next move, she wriggled her hips and was reprimanded with a hard slap on her bottom.

"Do I have your attention now?" He laughed.

"Sorry," she giggled. Elated that she'd fed from Anthony, she allowed herself to relax into submission. No matter what he'd ask, she'd give it to Kade.

"You're magnificent, my little vamp," he praised. "Look what you did to our poor detective. He can barely move."

"No pain," she grunted. Flesh meeting flesh resounded throughout the room as he pounded into her. The smell of sex permeated her nose and her core clamped down around Kade's cock.

"No pain. Only pleasure. You did that."

"I did that..." Her words trailed off as he slammed into her again.

"We did that. You and I." He dug his fingers into her hair, fisting it.

The sting of her hair being pulled reminded her that she was as alive as before she'd been turned. Kade, her husband-to-be, master of her body's pleasure, had done what he'd promised. She'd survived and he'd never leave her unprotected.

With her head tilted back, she was able to catch a hint of Anthony's smile as he enjoyed the show. Deferring to Kade, she surrendered to her own desire to be watched.

"Yes," she breathed, unable to speak the words that eluded her.

"You're mine, Sydney. From that very first day we met." He reached underneath and cupped her breast, pinching her nipple between his fingers. "You are everything to me."

"Always." She was overcome with emotion; tears brimmed through her lashes as her climax teetered on the precipice of its explosion.

"Whatever you need, I will always give it to you."

"Please...I can't wait, harder," she pleaded.

Kade plunged into her, over and over, increasing the pace. Her pussy convulsed around him as he stroked the strip of nerves inside her core with the tip of his cock. The first wave of her climax tore through her and she screamed his name at the top of her lungs. The sound of his grunting drove her to widen her stance, welcoming every hard thrust he gave. As he came, she fell onto her stomach and he rolled her onto her side, while still quietly pumping into her.

"I love you," he told her, grazing his lips against her hair.

"I love you so much. What you did for me...I'm sorry

about everything. I should have trusted you."

"Shh, my sweet little vampire. You're going to be all right. It's all going to be all right."

Kade pulled a sheet over her, shielding her nude body from Anthony's view and Sydney suspected he hadn't planned to share her any further than he had. What he'd done was only to ensure that she be able to learn to feed, to give and receive pleasure within the safety of his presence.

Anthony tied his pajama pants and shoved himself out of bed. As he went to walk away, their eyes locked and she mouthed the words, 'thank you'. He gave her a wink and left her and Kade alone. What had happened between the three of them had forever changed her life; she'd now be able to control the sensations caused by her bite, giving her independence.

As darkness fell, Sydney reveled within the warmth of Kade's loving embrace. In the morning they'd face a killer, but in the heat of the night, they'd celebrate their love. No longer drifting apart, their passion and devotion to each other had withstood the impossible. Tomorrow, healed, they'd go after Pat Scurlock and Sydney swore to herself that this time when she found him, he wasn't going to be leaving New Orleans alive.

✥ *Chapter Ten* ✥

Kade kissed the nape of Sydney's neck, his arousal prodding her back. She moaned but didn't yet wake, and he recalled the events of the prior evening. The erotic exchange with Anthony had been an extraordinary success. Surprisingly, Kade hadn't felt jealousy as his fiancée pleasured another man. She'd shown restraint by going no further than touching Anthony, demonstrating the ability to control both her hunger and desire.

Thoughts of the killer infiltrated his mind. He had to identify the vampire who was aiding and abetting the escapee. It made no sense that a supernatural would allow a human to lead any kind of activity, let alone one of a criminal nature. He'd ordered Luca to take an account of every vampire in the city. With over two hundred in the surrounding parishes, it wouldn't take long to rule out the innocents, narrowing the others down to a short list. Whoever it was obviously hadn't been in the town very long. A bigger question was how they had a connection to Pat Scurlock.

Sydney stirred, and Kade spooned her, wrapping his arm around her waist. Despite the danger they faced, he wished he could stay like this forever. Within seconds his phone buzzed and he glanced to the bed stand, noting Luca's text. Without releasing his mate, he reached and touched a forefinger to its glass. He cursed as he read the message: *Problem at Sangre Dulce.*

Kade shook his head and rolled away from Sydney. With no time to waste, he headed toward the bathroom. He'd let her sleep for a few more minutes before their hunt continued.

The odor of smoke hung thick in the air as Sydney carefully navigated through the charred remnants of what used to be Sangre Dulce. It had been months since she'd been there. At one time, it housed a mixed venue for kink lovers, both humans and supernaturals alike. Unfortunately, it'd also been the scene where a former psychopath mage, Asgear, had chosen to target his victims. The dark club tended to attract both good and evil, experienced and neophytes, all congregating for the purpose of pleasure and pain.

She was focusing on looking for clues, when she caught sight of Kade in a heated discussion with Anthony. Her stomach fluttered as she recalled her evening with both men. She could have taken it further, she knew. The desire to make love to Anthony had been strong. She and Kade had talked about the experience in detail on the way over in the car. She'd been afraid to admit her feelings, but he'd assured her she'd done well. Sexual arousal was an illusion, one that could be controlled. She suspected she'd want to drink from Anthony again, but knew she'd never fall in love with anyone but Kade. He was her universe and reason for living, every breath she took was a dedication to their love.

The sound of her foot breaking through a piece of soggy wood drew her focus back to the scene. *Why did Pat Scurlock burn down Sangre Dulce?* Kidnapping and torture were the hallmarks of his crimes, not arson. Pat had always resorted to all too common ways of selecting his victims, such as trolling mall parking lots for women who shopped alone. She considered that maybe he was trying to kill a vampire. Torching the building would certainly have done the trick. But according to the firemen, Sangre Dulce was closed when the fire started; no human bodies had been found. Sydney kicked at the soot beneath her feet. Ash was ash. If a vampire had been killed, the fragments stuck to her boots could be the disintegrated remains of vampire. No one would ever know.

"Maybe you and Anthony should go get some coffee," Kade suggested, startling her.

"I know you're worried and I love you for it, but seriously, I'm okay," she assured him.

"You let me know if you get hungry. No more dizzy spells. I've got donors on call." He glanced at Anthony, who approached. "The detective is still here for you, too."

"Thanks." She smiled and reached for his hand. "I'm doing well. I think last night…"

"Hey," Anthony said, a warm smile crossing his face.

"Hey, yourself," Sydney said. "I was just telling my fiancé here that I feel great. About last night…I know I already thanked you, but it meant everything to me…to us. I'm feeling like a new woman."

"It was pretty hot, huh?" Anthony teased. "Who knew getting bitten could be so much fun?"

"Don't get used to it, my friend," Kade warned with a wink to Sydney. "On second thought, Sydney may need some practice."

"Now, now, boys. We did have fun, but it may have been a one-time kind of thing."

Both men feigned saddened expressions and she laughed. "Okay, maybe a couple more times, but I can't keep Tony in New Orleans forever."

"I won't lie. It was pretty awesome. You think Philly's got any hot vamp women?"

"I'm sure Tristan could hook you up in his club," Sydney replied.

"Tristan is the only one I'd trust with our detective's safety." Kade's face dropped as he spoke.

"What's wrong?" Sydney asked.

"Everyone quiet!" Kade yelled. "Shh…"

"What is it?" Anthony whispered.

"Shh." Kade held up a hand, silencing them.

Not a sound but the whoosh of passing cars could be

heard in the room. In the distance, a baby cried.

"I thought I heard footsteps…something." He shook his head in confusion and waved Luca over. "I want you to stay here with Anthony."

"But Kade…" Sydney began.

"No arguments, love. If there're any surprises in the back rooms, Luca and I will ferret them out."

"Both P-CAP and the firemen have been through this building. It should be safe." As much as she tried to rationalize what she was saying, the same instinct that had always kept her alive told her something was off.

"Safe or not, I agree with Kade. You'd better stay with me," Anthony insisted.

"I know, it's just that I don't want him going alone."

"I'm going with him, darlin'. I promise we'll be back in a few minutes." Luca rested his palm on her shoulder.

There was a time she and Luca had fought like cats and dogs. But their relationship had evolved into one of respect and friendship. They lived on the same property and Sydney had become close with his fiancée, Samantha, a witch, who was expecting.

"Okay, but both of you better be careful. You've got a baby on the way, big man. No messing around, you hear me? Call us if something happens," she told him.

"Whatever the noise was I don't hear it now," Kade lied. He leaned in and pressed his lips to hers. "I promise we'll just have a quick look."

"Be careful."

"I'll be right back." Kade's eyes met Anthony's.

"Detective?"

"We'll kick around in here, check out what's left of the bar and kitchen."

Kade nodded and took off through the rubble. Luca shoved away debris that blocked the entrance and they disappeared into the darkness. Sydney bit her lip, wrapping her arms around her waist. Never in her life had she considered herself 'needy'. She wasn't sure if it was their bond strengthening, perhaps caused by Kade turning her, but without him near, her stomach churned in worry. Resisting the urge to cry, she took a deep breath and allowed Anthony to take her into his arms. *Bawling at a crime scene is not an option*, she thought. *Get your shit together.*

Within minutes, she'd calmed her emotions, cognizant that with her transition, she had to learn how to better control her primal impulsivity. Ready to resume her work, she broke out of Anthony's arms and pointed to the bar. In silence they picked through the remnants. She found herself looking back toward the hallway where Kade and Luca had gone. No matter the reassuring silence, she teemed with restless worry. Scurlock's motives for burning the club to the ground may have been nebulous, but Sydney was certain he'd been the one who had done it.

Anthony called for her to go into the kitchen and she nodded. Her cell phone buzzed and she retrieved it from her pocket. By the time she'd finished reading the text from Mya's number, the color had drained from her face. *495809 Mattise Lane 9pm* The hair on the back of her neck stood up as Luca's voice reverberated throughout the musky air. Without giving it a second thought, she sprinted through the pitch black hallway toward the back of the club. Suspecting something had happened to Kade, she ignored Anthony's calls for her to return.

Kade speculated that Sydney's senses were becoming more sensitive, but she hadn't yet developed them enough to hear the soft crunch of the embers in the alleyway. Both he and Luca had heard footsteps, but as they made their way down the hallway, they were met with dead silence. Kade reasoned that it could have been looters, but his instincts told him that danger lurked in the darkened sex rooms. As they moved further into the labyrinth, it became apparent that the fire hadn't progressed past the bar and seating area. He ran his finger along the soot-covered wall, its smooth texture sticking to his skin. The plastered structure remained firm as he rapped it with his knuckles.

Luca passed to his right and he nodded, acknowledging his departure into a larger room. Several feet up he spotted a door to a private alcove. The claustrophobic area housed just enough room for two lovers to engage in what surely would be an intense encounter. Approximately five by five feet, there was little room to wield a whip. While many of the spaces encouraged exhibitionism and voyeurism, this tiny closet did not allow for observation.

Kade wrapped his fingers around the cool brass doorknob and turned it. A loud click gave way to silence. He glanced over his shoulder, checking behind him. Confident no one was following, he placed a foot through its entrance. Scanning the room, he saw no other doors. A cool breeze grazed his face, and he caught sight of a small piece of cardboard fluttering in the wind. His attention was drawn upward to a large hole in the ceiling. The heart-shaped paper had been wound around a metal ring which was attached to the concrete wall. With both caution and curiosity, Kade approached. He took it between his fingers, noticing that unlike everything else in his surroundings, it was dry as a bone. He flipped it over, and saw the message: *She's dead.*

By the time he heard the door slam shut, the heavy silver chain had fallen onto him. He swatted at it, the stench of scorched skin permeating the room. It fell away to the floor but his reprieve was brief. Kade grunted as a wooden dart pierced deep into his thigh.

"Luca!" He yanked the splintered projectile from his flesh.

A hidden door slid open and a blinding stream of light speared into his eyes. As the first human came at him, he swung, landing a solid punch to his face. A second chain wrapped around his neck, and he struggled to free himself. He fell to his knees, clawing at the interwoven rings. His head smashed against pavement as they dragged him into the van. A tunnel of darkness closed in, and his final thoughts were of Sydney.

Chapter Eleven

"Where's Kade?" Sydney cried. Luca blocked her from entering the room where Kade had disappeared, and she pounded on his chest. "You fucking said you'd keep him safe."

"We'll find him," Luca told her.

"What happened? Where is he?" She pushed around Luca and stumbled into what remained of the room. She caught sight of the large breach in the ceiling and wall. She ran into the alleyway, and looked up and down the street.

"We got a number on the car," Anthony offered, coming up behind her.

"You didn't answer me." She confronted Luca. "How could you let this happen?"

"I was in the other room. There was no one back here. I swear it," he explained, raking his fingers through his hair. "When I heard him yell, I ran down the hallway and he was gone. You know we're like humans during the day. I can't chase down a car."

"Are you fucking serious?" she growled. He attempted

to reach for her and she broke free of his hold. "Don't touch me. That is it. I'm done with this bullshit. Look at this." She held up her phone, showing him the text.

"What?"

"The time and address. Tonight. He wants me to come alone." She laughed. "I'm going all right. By the time I'm done with him, he'll wish he'd stayed in that shithole prison."

"Syd," Anthony began.

"No. Don't say anything, Tony. He's fucking dead. This," she hissed, allowing her fangs to drop. She gestured to her mouth and then to Luca who'd also exposed his teeth, "is who I am now. I'm not human anymore. I may have lived by human rules before, but those days are gone."

"But…"

"She's right," Luca interjected.

"Last night you saw the best of me, but deep inside there's a monster that's going to be let loose. Every single human and vampire involved with taking Kade is going to die. You can either help or leave, but you will not stop me."

"Sydney, you know I'll always have your back…it's just…" Anthony stammered.

"Tony. Please just stop. Are you with me? 'Cause I know for damn sure Luca's coming."

"Fuck yeah," Luca agreed.

"This asshole thinks that I'm weak…that I can't feed because he's got Mya. He thinks that because he took

Kade, he owns me. But he's so fucking wrong," she growled. "He's mine."

Sydney took a long draw of blood from Anthony's wrist while he lay back on the sofa. She'd been so concerned that she'd lose control that she insisted that Luca and Samantha stay with her in the room. After fainting in Mya's apartment, she was determined to feed more often and stay strong. Concentrating, she'd focused like Kade had taught her. Reaching within her mind, she focused on knowing he was her friend, that she'd never hurt him. She cut off all sexual thoughts, but still ensured it was pleasurable for Anthony.

As she released Anthony's arm, she felt a small comforting hand on her shoulder and glanced up at Samantha. The red-haired witch was full with child, and they expected she'd go into labor within the month.

"You did nicely," she said softly.

"Thanks, Sam. You okay?" Sydney asked Anthony. Relief poured through her as his eyes flickered open and he gave her a grin.

"Yeah, I'm good."

"Thank God," she sighed.

"Not as good as last night, but with the big man out..."

"Don't even joke about it."

"We're going to find him."

"I know, but right now, I can't think of anything else but getting Kade home safe."

"He's a strong vampire." Samantha sat down next to Sydney and took her hand. "And you're strong too. I can see it in your aura. Everything has changed. You and Luca can do this."

"Hey, what about me? I'm startin' to feel a little underappreciated here." Anthony inspected his forearm and rubbed his fingers over the newly formed skin.

"You're human. You must be careful," Samantha noted.

"The humans never understand how truly weak they are," Luca added, brushing his hand over Samantha's hair. "It'd be comical if it weren't so pathetic."

"Hey," Samantha scolded, glaring at the father of her child. "Not nice."

"But true," he countered.

"Still not nice. You're going to have to learn some manners when our daughter is born."

"I'll teach her how to fight off the vampires who seek to court her."

"She'll be able to fight them off herself with magic. Now, don't distract me." Her eyes darted over to Anthony, who looked amused by their exchange. "Even though Anthony is human, he can still help. But he must be extra cautious. Remember, dear, I was able to defend myself."

"But you were a witch when you did that. When you

were mortal…darlin', you know that didn't turn out so well."

"True, but Sydney was the one who saved me," Samantha countered. "And she was human when she did it. Now she's like you. And more determined than ever."

"Thanks for sticking up for me, ma'am, but I'm going no matter what these vamps say. I may not be all badass like Luca the Drac, but I'm a sharp shooter. I'm good with a stake too, if I must say. Been trainin' at home."

"You're not serious." Sydney shook her head.

"Like a heart attack. I just need a glass of juice and I'm gonna be ready to go here."

"Do you feel okay?" Sydney asked again, her voice soft with concern. She placed her palm to his cheek. "Did I take too much? I'm really sorry. I thought I only took a little bit…"

"I'm fine. It's like blood bank day at the station. Although I could use a cookie. Maybe a kiss to make it feel better." He waggled his eyebrows at her and she slapped his arm.

"Stop trying to distract me. If anything happens to you tonight, I'll never forgive myself."

"Ah, as much as I detest humans, I must give credence to the detective's courage," Luca said, giving Samantha a smile.

"He's going." Sydney blew out a breath and shook her head. "Dominique and Xavier stay home with Samantha."

"I don't need them," Samantha protested. "I'm well able to take care of myself."

"No arguments, darlin'. You and our baby are my world right now. Whoever did this will suspect I'm going with Sydney. They'll know you're alone."

"Sam, I know how it is to feel a little…" Sydney searched for another word besides helpless. It wasn't that Samantha didn't have powers, but they couldn't put her in jeopardy. She already had difficulty walking the distance between their homes. "…vulnerable. I know you got magic, girl, but with the baby? No…just no."

"Hell no," Luca added.

Samantha looked to Anthony, who shrugged.

"Sorry. Gotta agree with the two of them on this one. This is getting ugly and the last thing we need to do is put your baby in danger."

"What about Logan? He could go with you," Samantha suggested.

"That's a good idea. I'll give him a call on the way over. As wolf, it's likely they'll go undetected," Sydney agreed. She glanced at the address on her phone one more time and flashed it at Luca. "This is in St. Tammany Parish?"

Luca checked the screen. "Yeah. Not too far out of the city."

"As soon as the sun falls, we're outta here." Sydney shoved out of her chair, twisting her hair up into a knot. She dug a rubber band out of her jeans and made quick work of tying it up into a bun. "Weapons?"

"Yes, weapons," Luca repeated. "If there's one thing I have, it's those."

"I thought vamps didn't need guns," Anthony jibed.

"Just because I don't need them doesn't mean I don't like them." The corner of Luca's lip curled upward.

Sydney ignored their banter. Her thoughts drifted to Kade and her chest tightened. She knew Pat sought to punish her in the worst possible way, to inflict immeasurable pain by taking the one she loved. She closed her eyes, taking a deep cleansing breath in an attempt to focus on her task. Whatever went down tonight, she'd kill Pat Scurlock. The beast inside her would seek its revenge and she'd allow it its due. A night of reckoning would come, as her true nature was revealed.

The gravel beneath the tires spit up onto the car, cracking the windshield. The sound of the splintering glass should have startled Sydney, but she remained focused. From the satellite image, they determined that the secluded home was set deep into the forest. The lush landscaping had been well kept, indicating the property wasn't abandoned. It belonged to one D. Tessa Saulnier.

Luca had scoured the security records, and no person of that name was a registered vampire, nor had Logan heard of her. They assumed the individual was human, but neither Sydney nor Anthony could find any connection between the prior murders, Pat Scurlock and the home. They'd considered the possibility that perhaps there was a relationship between Scurlock and Saulnier. Yet with no evidence to prove it, they surmised it was more likely that Pat had broken into the home while Ms. Saulnier was on vacation. Repeated attempts to call the phone number on record were ignored, as were the several texts Sydney had sent to Mya.

Sydney choked on the dust streaming into her open car window. She glanced at Luca, who quietly nodded, then set his eyes back on the road. The click of Anthony's Sig Sauer told her he'd begun checking his weapon. It was a nervous habit she'd watched him do many a time when they worked together. Sliding the clip out and working the action, he made sure the weapon was loaded. Oddly, she found the sound of snapping metal comforting. They'd started this case together, arresting a murderer, and tonight she planned to end it.

"Here," Luca said, pointing to an entrance that sat fifty feet up the road.

He pulled the car over into the grass, got out and slid into the back seat with Anthony. Sydney jumped over the console and sat in the driver's seat. The large SUV's tinted windows blocked the view from outside, so only the faint outline of a driver could be seen inside the vehicle.

"We do this like we planned," Sydney told them. "I go in first. I'm who they want. Tony, you go around back with Luca. Get Kade before you come for me. If Mya's still alive…"

"Doubtful," Anthony stated. "It's been more than twenty-four hours. There's a good chance he's killed her by now."

"I have to agree with the detective."

"Like I said, Kade's the priority. Once you get him freed, come help me. If by some miracle Mya's still alive, we'll try to get her out."

"I'm not thrilled about this plan." Luca shook his head and placed his palm on her shoulder. "If something happens to you, Kade's going to kill me."

"Luca," Sydney began. She caught the flicker of his eyes in the rearview mirror. "We already went through this. I'll be the first to admit it; this half-baked plan of ours sucks, but we don't have any options. If they see you or if you try to go in after me, they're going to kill him. Knowing Scurlock, he's got him in the basement cuffed and silvered, with someone waiting on standby to stake him."

"He'll try to do Kade before he does her," Anthony noted. "He's keepin' him alive. He wants her to watch when he kills him. It's all part of the high …getting off while his vics cry and plead. He's got a hard on for torture, I'm tellin' ya, man."

"As soon as I'm in the house and the door shuts, you go round to the back. If for some reason they rush us, we go balls out with fire power and hope to hell that we make it. But that is like plan Z as far as I'm concerned. I'm not gonna park too close to the house. I'll run up to the door to keep the focus on me. Hopefully, they won't try to search the car. If they try to, I'll make a scene, and they'll take me inside faster."

"This is some fucked up shit, Syd. We don't even have backup," Anthony said.

"Logan will be around," Sydney reminded him.

"If things go south in the first two minutes, they'll join the party. But they won't get involved right away," Luca cautioned. "If we can handle this on our own, that's best. The last thing we need is to be responsible for one of the Alpha's wolves getting hurt, or worse, dying on us."

"Remember, take the path around to the back door. It used to be his M.O. to chain up his vics in the basement but we don't know what we've got going on here. This is Louisiana, so if there's no basement, he could be in the garage. He doesn't like to make a mess in the main living areas. When we caught the son-of-a-bitch, you would have thought he had a maid, it was so clean in there." Sydney patted Luca's hand and then turned the keys in the ignition. She kept the lights off and put the car in gear. "He's not going to kill me right away. This asshole wants retribution. But he'll want to torture me first. If I can keep him talking long enough for you to get Kade, then we have a chance. You need to find him."

"We'll get him, Syd," Anthony assured her.

"Once we get Kade, we're taking everyone out," Luca told him.

"Scurlock is mine," Sydney reminded them, her voice cold and even.

"Anthony, if we run into any trouble, let me handle it," Luca ordered. "No heroics, you hear me?"

"Jesus, you vampires are bossy. I think I can handle it.

We're the ones who got Scurlock the first time."

"Well, he's out now, so as far as I'm concerned humans created this shit show. What I say goes."

"Hey, chill. Save that testosterone. In a few minutes, you'll be able to kick as much ass as you want," she promised.

The conversation died as they approached their destination. She turned into the entrance, noting the huge decorative pillars that loomed on the corners of the property. Ominous gargoyles sat atop their stone perches, warning visitors of the impending danger that awaited them. She slowly navigated the winding herringboned driveway which was lined with Southern magnolia trees. In the distance a light flickered on the porch of the restored colonial revival mansion. Modernized, its exterior appeared freshly painted, its elaborate landscaping illuminated with spotlights. Two Mercedes sedans sat parked in the circle. Instead of driving through the carport, she opted to turn the car around so it was facing the street.

"You guys ready to rock and roll?" Sydney whispered. "'Cause I've got dinner waiting and this one's going down screaming."

She didn't bother waiting for a response as she exited. The front door flew open, and two large men wearing suits came toward her. Their leather masks, while distracting, did little to intimidate her. Showing no fear, she didn't resist as a pair of meaty hands dug into her forearm and hauled her into the house. As she stumbled into the foyer, the stench of cigarettes wafted into her nostrils, and she remembered that Pat was a chain smoker.

Sydney took note of the condition of the home's interior as her captors guided her into a large living room. From its impeccable cherry hardwood floors, to its ornate crown moldings, to the oriental carpets, the luxurious décor had gone unmarred. In the corner, a thick plastic tarp was spread across the floor. Mya's lifeless form lay wedged in the corner, blood splattered around her in speckled flecks. Blindfolded, her wrists tied with a belt, she'd been dressed in a black satin corset. Sydney caught sight of red panties that peeked through a long white tutu. A heavy black leather collar coiled around her neck. Several puncture wounds lined her pale shoulder and Sydney inwardly cringed, knowing she'd been violated. Despite the deadly silence, Sydney breathed in relief as she heard the shallow thump of Mya's heartbeat.

"Mya." Sydney wrenched her arm away from the guard and ran to Mya, her preternatural strength no match for the humans.

She reached for the weapon in her holster and fired off two shots. The bullets whizzed through the air, cleanly piercing through the leather that covered their foreheads. A trace of recognition that she'd just killed two criminals without thought as to whether or not they had a weapon on them flittered through her mind, but the animal inside her would seek a justice of its own. No longer encumbered by human law, she'd seek retribution without guilt.

"It's okay," Sydney assured Mya as she removed the

bindings from her wrists. She studied the leather choker, looking for its buckle. As she ran her fingers around the back of Mya's neck, she discovered the small metal studs and rectangular battery. She stifled her disgust and removed the electrocution device, revealing angry flesh burns. "Oh my God, what the hell…"

"No," Mya moaned, to Sydney's relief.

"Hey, Mya. It's Sydney. Remember me from the club?" she asked.

Sydney heard footsteps behind her and went to turn but was too late. The nightmare she'd put away behind bars stood in the vestibule pointing his gun at them. Out of the corner of her eye, she caught the glare of the red laser dot on Mya's forehead.

"Long time no see, detective," he sneered.

"What do you want?" Sydney asked, already knowing full well he wanted her. She prayed Luca and Anthony had found Kade, but until they arrived, she'd have to hold her own.

"I've been waiting for so long, it almost feels like Christmas," he chuckled.

Sydney observed his appearance, noting that he'd lost weight. While still tall in stature, his gangly legs swam in his jeans, his thin tattooed arms poking through a muscle shirt. He looked as if he were a scarecrow, broomsticks for arms with not nearly enough straw stuffed into his middle. She knew better than to mistake his scrawny build for weakness. It was his mind, not his body that his victims feared.

Her heart began to race, anticipating the violence to come. The battle. His imminent death. She'd come to him as judge, jury and executioner and was prepared to carry out the sentence. But it would not come without cost.

"You shouldn't have come to New Orleans." She glanced to the gun in her hand.

"Drop it, detective." He swirled the red dot on Mya's skin, reminding her of his true hostage. "You can probably shoot me. You might even kill me, but I'll definitely kill her. Do you really want to be responsible for ending an innocent life?"

Sydney knew he'd murder Mya in a New York minute. She was certain he was waiting to parade a shackled Kade in front of her, his grand finale of torture. What she didn't know was if there were more victims in the house. She wished her supernatural senses would kick in so she could hear what was happening in the other parts of the house, but so far, her ears were almost as human as the murderer standing in front of her.

She slowly backed away from Mya. Pat would have to make a choice, her or the girl.

"No, no, no, detective," he chided. "Gun on the ground. Now."

Sydney forced a cold smile onto her face and gently laid the weapon down on the woolen carpet. Adrenaline pumped as she considered her next move. He took a step toward her, and she launched herself at Scurlock. As she tackled him to the floor, he fired off a shot. The slug whizzed by Mya's head, shattering a Tiffany lamp. Sydney ignored the exploding shards of colored glass and wrestled Pat onto his back. She pinned his wrists to the ground, and he spat at her face. The slimy sputum dripped down her temple, and she coughed at the foul-scented nicotine.

"Get off me, bitch!"

"You're dead," Sydney hissed. Her fangs lengthened as she tasted victory.

As she reared her head to bite him, a loud pop fired into the air, and the heat of a bullet sliced into her thigh. Although it pierced her flesh clean through, the silver metal poisoned her system and she was unable to hold onto her prey. Tears streamed down her face, as her back hit the wooden planks. Through the haze of the moisture, the outline of a woman came into view...*Mya.*

"I'm sorry," Mya mumbled. As if she were drugged, her words came out jumbled.

"Why?" Sydney wiped her face with the back of her hand, refusing to give in to the excruciating pain.

"I can't...he's always loved me...mother...mother needs him." The gun tumbled from Mya's hands and Pat shoved to his feet and grabbed her by the back of her neck.

"About time, you dumb bitch. She almost killed me. At least you didn't kill her." He dragged Mya over to the tarp and threw her to the floor.

Confused, Sydney tried to process what was happening. He'd abused Mya, yet she'd saved him. As she pushed up onto her elbows, Sydney heard the click of heels in the hallway. Tearing off her jacket, she wrapped it around her thigh in an attempt to stem the flow of blood pouring out from her wound. The tapping grew closer, and she sensed a vampire was near.

She crawled toward the wall and clutched at it, using it as leverage. But as she hoisted herself upward, she lost her footing and slipped in her own blood. She shoved onto her hands and knees, clawed at the chair rail and fought to right herself against the wall. Pat's maniacal laughter echoed in her ears. She knew he'd let her rally, to prolong her suffering. He'd allowed his victims to heal, even if it took weeks, so that he could torment them over and over.

Heaving for breath, she stared into his seething eyes as he fell back onto the sofa and chuckled. Pat waved the gun, his arms spread wide across the back of the couch. He broke eye contact, and Sydney turned to see who'd caught his attention. Her heart dropped as the vampire entered the room, holding the victim by the back of her hair. Sydney released a cry she hadn't known she possessed as her eyes locked on Samantha's. With her mouth duct taped shut, she was unable to speak, and the tears in her eyes told Sydney that she was unable to use her magic.

"How could you do this?" Sydney exclaimed.

She moved to rescue Samantha, but the pain was too much. As her leg became numb, she shifted all her weight to one foot in an effort to stand.

"Hello, Sydney. We've been expecting you," the vampire told her.

"Kade's going to kill you." Sydney sucked a breath, summoning every last ounce of energy that remained.

The vampire merely laughed, throwing the pregnant

prisoner to the ground. Sydney fell reaching to catch Samantha. The shock of her leg hitting the floor shot a stabbing pain throughout her entire body. She grasped at the carpet, dragging herself over to her friend. When Sydney reached Samantha, she took her into her arms, and glared at her attacker. *Dominique.*

·❦· *Chapter Twelve* ·❦·

"I told you not to make a mess." Dominique glared at Pat.

"I swear I'll clean it up. It's her fault. Look what she made me do," he complained.

"You're a disgrace."

"No, stop saying that," he whined.

"Look what you did. All this blood wasted…"

"Let me kill her…she deserves to die. She put me away. She *ruined* my life."

"How can you do this?" Sydney interrupted their conversation.

"Shut up, bitch." He pointed the gun at her.

"There's still the matter of Issacson." Dominique smoothed a stray hair from her face and brushed a tiny speck of lint off her crisp white sleeve.

"I don't care anymore. I just want her dead."

"You never did master torture the way I taught you. Such a disappointment you are." Dominique glanced at Sydney, and gave a strong kick to her injured leg. Ignoring her cries, she approached Mya. "And her, she's never been anything. No matter how hard I've tried, she's failed me."

"If you'd just make us vampires, we wouldn't have to do this…"

"Silence, you idiot. The only reason I brought you down here…*allowed* you to come here into my home was to take her out." She pointed at Sydney. "And you haven't even done that right. Now look what you made me do."

"How could you do this?" Sydney couldn't fathom why Dominique would attack her. "I know we haven't always been friends but this isn't you."

"You don't even know who I am," she snapped.

"Why don't you tell me then, because Kade's going to be here soon and I'll tell you what, he's going to kill you… and him." She looked over to Pat.

"He's not going anywhere."

"Luca's going to find him and they'll be coming for you."

"Yeah well, not anymore. Once he sees that I've got his precious cargo on board, he'll leave Kade with me." Dominique spun and snatched a tissue out of her small purse. She knelt down and began to scour a tiny smudge of blood, which soon blended into a pink blob on the cream-colored carpet. "I can't believe you ruined my rug. It's an antique."

"I didn't mean to do it…accidents happen." Pat scrubbed the barrel of the gun against his chin.

"Must I do everything myself?" Dominique leaned over and grabbed Samantha by her arms, yanking her up to her feet.

"Mother," Pat declared, pushing off the sofa. "This is your responsibility."

Dominique is Pat Scurlock's mother? What the ever loving fuck? If she is his mother, then who is …? Sydney's eyes fell onto Mya, who'd fallen back into a drug-induced haze. Unresponsive, she lay passed out in the corner. Dominique laughed, and Sydney's attention was drawn back to the vampire who dangled Samantha like a rag doll. Shocked, she studied the red-haired vampire, who looked identical to her friend. *No, no, no. Dominique would not do this.*

Sydney focused on Pat as he crossed the room and approached the one he'd called Mother. Sydney began to feel dizzy; she'd lost too much blood. Her heart started to race. If she didn't feed soon, she'd pass out like she'd done in Mya's apartment. Her mind went fuzzy. As if she'd entered an alternative universe, she observed Pat take Dominique's free hand. He began to kiss it, not like a son, but as a lover. Sydney fought the bile that rose in her stomach. By the time his lips met Dominique's, Sydney's vision had begun to blur. She prayed to God that Kade and Luca would arrive soon. She wouldn't last much longer.

Kade's voice bellowed through the robin's-egg-blue steel cellar doors. Anthony secured his gun with both hands, keeping it upright. His heart pounded against his ribs in anticipation. Luca held his fingers to his lips and reached for the handle. Anthony had never been one to cower away from a dangerous situation, but he was well aware that he was no match for the supernatural forces that lay in wait. But having made a connection with Kade, he'd known he'd give his own life to save him.

The creaking storm door flew open, and within seconds he and Luca had broken down the oak door which stood as the home's last defense. As he stepped into the darkness, he choked on the stench of urine. Reaching for his small flashlight, he flicked it on and caught sight of Luca wrestling a vampire into the far corner of the basement. He swiveled to the right and spied a woman lying motionless on a stained futon. Her blouse had been torn open, her neck littered with small bites. Her eyes bulged, blindly staring into the rafters. Certain she was dead, he moved to Kade, who groaned his name.

"It's okay, man." Anthony stifled his reaction as he shone the light onto his friend. Tethered by silver to sewer pipes, Kade's pale skin had been marred with cigarette burns.

"Get me out of here," Kade pleaded; his voice, usually strong, wavered.

"How many are there?"

"Maybe four or five. I'm not sure."

"I got ya."

"Tony...there's a guard. Where's Luca?" Kade coughed, his chin lolling forward onto his chest.

"I'm good," Luca yelled from across the room. The clatter of wood breaking sounded in the corner.

"Is he smiling?" Kade joked.

"You know he loves a good ass kicking." Anthony couldn't believe Kade was making light of the situation, given his condition. He gingerly tried to remove the silver chains, but they'd been wound in knots, a padlock securing them in place. "You couldn't get tied up by something a little easier? Cuffs I could do. Rope even. But a fucking padlock? Jesus Christ."

"Stop complaining."

"Yeah, yeah, gotcha." Anthony laughed. He pushed up onto his feet, searching for a tool to open the lock. It wasn't lost on him that Kade had called him Tony. As long as he'd known him, Kade had maintained a formal disposition, one that set him apart from vampires and mortals alike. Anthony suspected that his vulnerability had altered his usual reserved demeanor, but he decided not to call attention to it. A loud grunt sounded from the corner, and he flashed the light over to Luca, who'd taken a right hook to his cheek. "You need some help over there?"

"Hell, no. We're just having a little fun." Luca dug his foot into the guy's chest, and sent him flying across the room. "Now would you stop jerkin' off over there and get Kade loose?"

"Goddamned fucking vampires." Anthony shoved boxes to the side, looking for something he could use as a tool. He picked up what he thought was a screwdriver but it was made out of plastic. Hurling it across the room, he spied what he needed in a cobwebbed corner. "The only reason I'm here is because Sydney was once human. A very nice human."

"We were all human once. Luca's right. Stop fucking around and get this off me," Kade goaded.

"Ungrateful motherfuck…" Anthony wrapped his hands around an axe and hauled it out of the debris. It lodged in the boxes, and he continued to yank it toward him until he broke it free.

"No need for name calling." Luca smashed an antique crib headboard over his knee, and broke a jagged shard off into his fist.

"Scurlock is human," Kade reminded him.

"Glass houses." Luca lunged at the vampire.

"Pot meet kettle." Kade spat up blood and a sickening gurgle came forth from his throat. His eyes fluttered shut.

"Fuck, no. Now, you listen to me, Kade. You're not going to die on me, man." Anthony rushed to Kade's side, tapping the side of his cheek with the palm of his hand. Pulling out the silver, he extended it far enough so he could break it off without snaring one of Kade's arms. He lifted the sharp instrument into the air and swung down hard. The metal sparked as the chain split open, and Kade's head slammed against the concrete floor. "Not on my watch."

"Shit." Anthony threw the axe onto the floor. Out of the corner of his eye he saw Luca staking the vampire. "About fucking time."

"What?" Luca asked breathlessly, his lips curled in victory.

"Help me. There's somethin' wrong with him." Anthony slid his hands under Kade's arms and dragged him into the middle of the room. He sat on the concrete, pulling his injured friend onto his lap. Cradling him, he shined the flashlight onto his skin and checked his pulse.

"He's gonna be fine," Luca assured Anthony. He knelt down and thumbed open one of Kade's eyelids. "He's gotta eat, though."

"I got this." Anthony rolled up a sleeve. "Check on the girl over there. I think she's dead."

"Aw, shit." .

"You know her?"

"Name's Gemma. Used to be a donor. She's gone."

"This isn't working." Anthony held his arm to Kade's mouth but he didn't move to feed.

"You aren't doing it right." Luca stood and towered above him. "Open his lips with your fingers. Put your skin right on his tongue. He's alive. He'll get the hint."

"I swear to God, I'm never hangin' out with the two of you again." Anthony reluctantly did as Luca told him. Recalling his reaction to Sydney's bite, he attempted to remain calm. He wasn't sure which would be worse, the sting or the ecstasy. He'd never been attracted to a man before but with Kade and Sydney, lines became blurred.

"You do realize Sydney's up there? Hurry up with it."

"Fuck off." Anthony sucked a breath as Kade's tongue traced a warm path along his wrist. His body jerked; fangs sliced into his skin. "Oh shit, oh shit, oh shit...ahh."

"Buck up. You humans are such weaklings," Luca

chastised with disdain.

"This is so wrong." The rush of pleasure overcame Anthony as Kade suctioned his blood. Masculine hands grabbed his forearm, tightening the seal on his flesh. His cock jerked in response and his eyes rolled up into his head. "Is it over yet? I can't do this. Come on, Kade. Are we good, man?"

"We're good," Kade breathed, licking at the wound.

"Hold on a second. Jesus," Anthony said, his semi-hard dick pressing at his zipper.

"Shake it off. Let's get moving." Kade jumped to his feet, energized by his feeding.

"Yeah, I'll get right to that." Anthony gingerly pushed to his feet and adjusted himself.

"I think your donor liked it," Luca noted.

"I'm not his fucking donor." Anthony pulled his shirt down over the bulge in his pants.

"Of course he liked it. They all like it when I do it." Kade smiled at Anthony and clapped his hand on his shoulder, then shoved him toward Luca.

"You guys are assholes, you know that, right?" Anthony retrieved his gun from its holster.

"We love you too." Kade moved to the stairs. "Now where the hell is my woman?"

"How do you know we let her come with us?" Anthony asked.

"I know my mate. There is no 'letting' Sydney do anything. I knew she'd come for me. It was just a matter of when." Kade ran up to her, his feet barely touching the steps.

Chapter Thirteen

A gunshot sounded and Kade tore through the house. As he rounded into the living room, confusion crossed his face. Dominique smiled coldly back at him, her arm wrapped around Samantha's neck. He held his hands up to halt Anthony from coming any further, but it didn't stop Luca from bursting past him.

"Don't move another step," Dominique sneered, her fangs inches from Samantha's neck. "I always enjoyed the taste of a pregnant woman. There's nothing like the innocence of the unborn."

"Get the fuck off her," Luca yelled.

"Dom. What's going on here?" Kade regarded her face. The woman before him looked like Dominique but the fine lines around her lips appeared deeper, as if she was a long time smoker.

His eyes fell to Sydney, who stared blankly back at him. Her sallow complexion indicated significant blood loss, and his anger spiked at the sight. A flicker of recognition flared in her eyes, and he suspected she was purposely feigning despondence.

"My son has a bone to pick with your fiancée…her bones," she laughed, tightening her grip on Samantha's neck. "And this witch? Pity she can't chant her mumbo jumbo with her mouth taped shut."

"Let her go," Luca demanded, taking a step toward her.

"Get back," she hissed. "This is between Patty and his detective. If you leave right now, I may let her go." She licked Samantha's neck clear up to her cheek and temple. "Or not." She gave a wicked smile and lapped at the skin. "I've forgotten how delicious witches can be. Mmm…I can taste the infant in her belly."

"No!" Pat waved his gun in the air. "Kade stays here. I want to play. You never let me play, mother."

"Only when you've earned it," she chided. "Look what you've done to my house. A punishment is in order."

"No!" He stomped his foot like a petulant child.

"All of you leave now, and the witch stays alive," she explained calmly.

"I'm not leaving you." Luca's eyes locked on Samantha's. She violently shook her head. Smothered garbled words came from underneath her gag.

"See? The little woman agrees with me," Dominique told him.

"I don't know who you are or what you did with Dominique, but you aren't her." Kade's fangs descended and he caught sight of Sydney reaching for her gun that had been tossed underneath the sofa.

"Clever, clever boy. Doesn't matter much what I am

now, does it? I hold the cards." With ease, her fangs pierced Samantha's creamy white flesh. Instantly, she retracted them, laughing as blood ran down her face. Samantha began to heave, the adhesive gag restricting her breathing.

"Stop, you're hurting her. Take me," Luca pleaded, inching closer.

"Tsk, tsk, tsk…you've always been a killjoy, Macquarie." She licked her lips and glanced at Pat and then to Sydney. "Kill her now. I'm bored."

"But mother…"

"No arguing," she spat at him. "No one better move to stop him or the witch dies too."

Pat slowly turned to Sydney, who raised her gaze to meet his. With his gun trained on her, he reached for her collar. Kade had seen her sneak her weapon behind her back, but he couldn't be sure that she had enough strength to use it. Sydney gave her attacker a bitter smile, her sharp teeth beckoning him. As he hauled her to her feet, she spun around and aimed at Dominique. Firing off a shot, she clipped her shoulder.

"No!" Pat backhanded Sydney across the face in response.

The sight of his mate being attacked sent Kade into a rage that was only slightly tempered when Sydney stood firm. Instead of faltering, she rebounded from the blow to her cheek and laughed at Pat's surprised expression. She lunged at him, pinning him onto his back. Kade made a move toward Pat, but Mya leapt to her feet, a knife in her hand. Her attempt to thwart him was interrupted as Anthony fired his weapon, his bullet slicing into her thigh. By the time Kade had reached Sydney, she had Pat's face wedged against the floor with her hand. Like a rabid dog, she'd gone feral, with her fangs poised to kill. Kade watched with pride as she took her prize, tearing her teeth into his flesh.

Maniacal laughter emanated from Dominique, and he caught sight of her dragging Samantha across the room. Holding Luca's gaze, she lodged her fangs in Samantha's shoulder. Luca charged and jammed his fingers up into Dominique's lips, trying to pry her jaw open, but like a vise, she tightened her bite. Kade slipped behind Dominique and dug his claws deep into her neck. She thrashed but didn't relent as his fingers strummed at her carotid. Extending his nail further, he sliced at it, sawing away the tendons that held it in place.

Blood streamed from the wound as she fought death. Kade closed his eyes, relieved when life drained from her body. She slumped in his arms, finally releasing Samantha into Luca's waiting embrace. Kade stumbled back onto the ground, carefully placing Dominique's limp form on the carpet. Drenched in her blood, he fought the regret that he hadn't helped her, stopped her from evolving into a debauched nightmare. Despite her identical appearance to Dominique, he still doubted that the life he had taken was that of his friend. Conflicted, his instincts warred with what appeared to be the reality of the situation.

Kade gazed over to Sydney, who wore a sympathetic

expression. Pat lay dead and mangled beside her. Physically, she'd healed herself, stealing his essence. Shoving off the ground, Kade went to her, carefully scooping her up into his arms. As her tears began to flow, he crushed her to his chest. The familiar scent of his mate calmed his beast, his fangs rescinding.

"It's okay, love," he whispered.

"He's dead."

"It's over." Kade's heart broke for her, aware that she was still far too human to go unaffected by her actions.

"I killed him…I knew I would but I feel…" she stammered.

"You did what you had to do. You knew this world…my world, it wasn't your own. But now, it is." A surge of guilt for changing her into a vampire rushed fresh through his mind. "I wish things were different."

"No, don't…don't apologize. Whatever just happened, I'd do it again. You're the only thing that matters to me…nothing else." As the shock wore off, she pushed away from Kade and scanned the room for Samantha. Her friend shook and cried within Luca's arms, but was still alive. Although Samantha was a witch and had the capability to heal herself, she'd been badly attacked. "Oh my God. Is she okay? The baby?"

"They'll both be all right, but I've gotta get her out of here," Luca responded.

"Thank God," she breathed in relief. "Where's Tony?"

In the melee, he'd gone missing, but Kade heard his voice coming from the hallway. He glanced over and caught him talking to Mya, who was laid out on the hardwood floor. Her eyelashes blinked but she wasn't verbally responding

"He's okay. He's right there," Kade growled.

"Mya... I don't understand what happened. I just don't know..."

"Don't know what?"

"How they're all linked together. Scurlock said Dominique was his mother. That makes no sense. And Mya...they knew her somehow. She shot me...protecting *him*. I don't get it. He tortured her. Why would she protect him? My God, you should see her neck." Sydney shook her head in confusion. She moved to go to Anthony but Kade wrapped his fingers around her wrists.

"Leave them. Tony can handle it." Kade intentionally held her back. While Sydney appeared to be calm, he was concerned she'd kill again.

"We can't just leave him."

"We'll text P-CAP. Look, Tony's cuffing her right now. She's not going anywhere."

"But we need to know why she did this."

"Soon enough, love. Right now, what we need to do is get home."

"And Dom...why would she do this? That woman...she looks like Dominique but it's crazy. Is that really her? Something is off here. I don't get it." Sydney rubbed her eyes with the back of her hand.

"We'll talk about it later." Kade still hadn't come to terms with the fact that he'd killed Dominique. It was out of character for her to commit such a heinous crime. Something about the way she talked, the slight changes to her skin was contrary to what he'd known for decades. He wondered if his mind was playing tricks on him, but like Sydney, he still had trouble believing it had been her.

"I know what you're thinking…. how else could she have gotten to Samantha? We need to talk to her and find out what happened," Sydney continued.

"Not now."

Sydney nodded in agreement, acquiescing to his suggestion. Kade stood and lifted her into his arms. On any other night, he'd stay and investigate, searching for a resolution to the unresolved questions that remained. Whatever answers they sought could wait until morning. Tomorrow was a new day, and the only thing he needed was to have his mate, to be lying in bed with her, in her, to claim her again.

Chapter Fourteen

The hot spray pelted her skin and she dipped her head forward. The wretched remains of death washed away down the drain with any remnants of regret she'd harbored. Reborn as vampire, she'd now live by Kade's law. Her decision made, she'd never return to the police force. She wasn't sure what she'd do moving forward, but she was certain her immortal life with Kade promised opportunities beyond her wildest comprehension.

Her thoughts turned to Samantha, who on the way home swore up and down that the red-haired vampire wasn't Dominique. As soon as they'd returned home, Samantha had been checked by the doctor, and neither she nor her baby had been seriously harmed.

Sydney had always known that as a vampire, Kade couldn't father a child. It was only through Samantha's magic that she and Luca had conceived. Recalling the demon's attack, Sydney held her hand to her belly, grieving for the child she'd only recently discovered she'd wanted. It was a bitter pill to swallow, knowing that she was physically incapable of bringing life into this world.

"You're thinking too hard, love," she heard Kade say as he rounded the glass enclosure, coming up behind her.

"I suppose I am," she replied.

"You upset about tonight?" he asked.

She moaned and laid the back of her head against his shoulder. His cock prodded her back, causing her to smile. Even when her mood had soured, Kade could lift her spirits.

"Hmm…no answer?" He kissed her temple.

"Just thinking," she hedged.

"About tonight?"

"Samantha and her baby. Ava, too."

"The Alpha's child? Were you thinking about the demon?" He paused. "The night you were attacked?"

"Maybe. No. I don't know…just about babies, period." Sydney held her breath as Kade's silence hung in the air.

"Wait." Kade spun her around in his arms. He took her chin into his hands and guided it upward until her eyes met his. "We haven't talked about this very often. I always assumed…"

Sydney gave him a small smile. She found it amusing that he was searching for words to articulate what he suspected.

"No…you never wanted any…Are you trying to tell me…?"

"I don't know…just forget it," she lied. Attempting to look away, her effort was thwarted as his hold grew tighter.

"Look at me, Sydney."

She did as he said, her heart pounding in her chest. *Is he angry with me? I should never have brought it up.*

"Do you want a child?" Kade asked softly. He released his tight grip, sliding his fingers upward to caress her cheek.

Sydney pressed her face into his palm, accepting his comfort. She nodded, closing her eyes. It broke her heart to come to this realization at a time in her life when it was no longer a possibility. Tears brimmed, and she lifted her lids, meeting his gaze.

"Don't cry…it's okay."

"But I shouldn't want this…it's not fair to you."

"Hey now, just because I never said I wanted a child with you didn't mean that I didn't want one. The only thing that's mattered is being with you." His lips grazed her forehead. "I've been alone for what seems like forever. And when you came along…Goddess, I just couldn't have been more shocked. You breathed life back into me."

"But…"

"Let me finish. When you said you didn't want kids, it was a relief to me only because I knew I couldn't give them to you, but never because I wouldn't want you to carry my child. If you'd told me you wanted a baby when we'd first met, I wouldn't have pursued you. I wouldn't steal your right to have children from you."

"I didn't want kids. It's just being around Ava and seeing Samantha all these months. I can't explain it." Flustered by her own feelings, she struggled to express why she'd changed her mind.

"Six months ago, you were a young woman who had options. People grow, Sydney. Not all people know they want children. Sometimes we change, our priorities change."

"I feel like I should have known. But I'm a different person now."

"It's natural to want more. I want more. I regret we waited to get married and I want to do it…as in yesterday."

She laughed and slid her palms up his chest.

"I'm not joking. Who knew this was going to happen this week? Some asshole comes back and tries to murder you. I could've died too. I'm not saying it's going to happen again, I'm just saying we've got to live life as if we were human…as if this day could be our last. We're not terribly immortal when staked. No matter how much we'd like to predict the future, that isn't one of our abilities."

"I wish."

"Yeah, me, too. So that's why I want to get married this week. No waiting."

"Okay." Kade never ceased to amaze her with his decisiveness. Even if she wanted to, she couldn't deny him.

"And after that, we can figure out this baby thing."

"But we can't…"

"We couldn't have kids when you were a human, but maybe there's something we can do. Look at Samantha and Luca…they're pregnant."

"But she's a witch."

"True. But even vampires hold a little magic. Sam might be able to help us. We can ask Léopold too. Just because I haven't heard of it ever happening, doesn't mean it doesn't exist. I'm old, but not nearly as old as him. He'll help. And if they can't help us, there're people…you know, agencies who can help us."

"Adoption?"

"Of sorts. Not human of course, but there are all kinds of beings around us, love. And not everyone is ready or wants to be a parent. It's an option."

"Are you serious?" Sydney asked. Her heart felt as if it'd burst from the hope he'd given her.

"Completely."

"I love you so much," she cried, squeezing him tight.

"I love you, too." He raked his fingers up into the wet strands of her hair, bringing her lips to meet his. "No more tears. We got this."

"Yes…"

Breathless, she welcomed his tongue as it swept against her own. Her nipples stabbed into his muscular chest as he commanded her body. Strong hands gripped her thigh, wrapping it around his waist. The cool tiles against her back contrasted with the explosive heat that grew between their slick bodies. Delirious from his kiss, she rocked her aching pussy against his leg. She bit at his lips, and reached for his rigid shaft, her fingers teasing its crown. Before she had a chance to stroke him, he'd dropped to his knees, nudging her open with his firm shoulder.

"Wider." Kade's fingers flittered over her hipbone.

Obeying, she stepped aside, giving him full access. Her heart raced as his eyes flickered to red before focusing on his task. The first lash of his tongue to her clit startled her and she reached for his head to steady herself.

"Don't move," he ordered, his warm breath teasing her pussy.

The dominating tone of his voice spiked her arousal and she whimpered as he sucked her sensitive nub into his mouth. His fingernails scraped her bottom, crushing her mound to his face. He feasted upon her, and she shuddered as his fingertip teased her entrance.

"Kade," she breathed.

"Tonight," he swiped at her clit with his flat tongue, "we begin anew."

"Yes, that's it." Her hips tilted forward, her body trembling as he plunged two fingers inside her. She rose onto the balls of her feet, the rush of orgasm shaking her to her core.

"Hmm." He hummed at her lips, flicking her swollen pearl and sucking it into his mouth.

"Ah yeah…like that. Oh, fuck, don't stop. Yes, yes," she screamed. Heaving for breath, her body fell limp as the waves of climax rolled through her.

Giving her no time to recoup, he spun her around and bent her at the waist so her ass was exposed to him. She trembled in anticipation. More than needing to be possessed, she sought to lose herself in the ecstasy of all that was her mate.

She groaned aloud as he buried himself inside her from

behind, filling her to the hilt. With her palms flat on the misty wall, she braced herself for each forceful thrust, the sound of his flesh slamming against hers. The sweet prick of his fangs at her shoulder held her in place, reminding her to be ever mindful of the moment. His warm lips on her skin, the scent of him in the air while wrapped in his strength overwhelmed her.

"So hard…yes!" She gave a cry of pleasure as he fucked her with unrestrained fervor.

"Ah yeah. Jesus, you feel good."

"Don't. Ever. Stop."

"This is only round one, baby," he teased.

"You promise?" He pounded into her, and she cried out loud. "Ahh."

"You have no idea. Plus, you owe me a spanking for coming to get me by yourself."

"What?" Her pussy tightened around him at the thought of it. Sydney submitted to no one….except Kade.

"You heard me." He scraped his sharp teeth across her pale skin. Drawing a bubbling line of blood, he lapped at it with his tongue.

"Yes…please," she cried, the sweet pain of his fangs at her neck.

"I love the sound of you begging," he grunted, slamming into her. Reaching to her breast, he pinched her ripe tip.

"Please, Kade…ahh." The twinge on her nipple sent a jolt straight to her core. She gasped, attempting to stem her orgasm.

"Please what?" He laughed, knowing he couldn't hold back much longer.

"Bite me…Just do it…Please."

"Since you asked so nicely." Without further warning, he struck, his teeth penetrating deep into her shoulder.

Sydney screamed, shuddering as the ripples of ecstasy tore through her. Limp against the wall, she panted; intense spasms consumed her.

Obsessed with her happiness, Kade plunged into his mate. Drinking in her delicious essence, he groaned as he came inside her. As his pulsating release subsided, he rejoiced in victory. His mate reclaimed, life was complete.

Chapter Fifteen

Sydney stirred in Kade's arms. Asleep, he gently snored and she smiled. Renewed with hope, her chest constricted with love. The man who owned her heart had given her life again, never giving up on her, even when she'd wanted to give up on herself.

She moved to leave the bed, and a gentle arm pulled her back inside the warm confines of the sheets.

"Where do you think you're going?" he asked.

"Nowhere," she giggled.

"Liar."

"I just wanted to see what Tony was doing."

"Ah…leaving me for another man?" His eyes narrowed, but the lilt of his smile told her he was joking.

"Not on your life."

"I couldn't share you." He twirled his forefinger into her hair.

"You don't have to. Our time with Tony…you know how I feel about him, but he's not you." She kissed him lightly on his chest.

"We can still play with him every now and then, though," He raised a playful eyebrow at her. "That is, if that's something you desire."

"You do surprise me, Mister Issacson." Kade had always pushed her sexually, testing the limits of where she'd find her greatest pleasure.

"I enjoy the detective's company. He'll leave us soon, but he was there for you...for me. We owe him," Kade added, his tone serious.

"He's true blue. Always has been," she told him. "But you're right...he's going home soon. We'll need a donor."

"I don't want strangers in between us."

"We can find someone we both like. Many someones, perhaps. But for food only, nothing more."

"Agreed."

"Thank you for understanding." She smiled, relieved that he didn't want to have a sexual relationship with donors. It wasn't as if he'd ever asked. But after what they'd done with Anthony, she'd wondered about his expectations.

A knock sounded and Kade drew the sheet over his mate's bared breasts.

"Come in," he called.

Anthony sheepishly entered the room, his gaze averted. Sydney laughed, realizing he was still unsure of how to proceed with their relationship. She was relieved when Kade broke the ice.

"Come sit, my friend." Anthony went to the chair across the room and Kade waved him over to the bed and patted the comforter. "Here."

Anthony shook his head and smiled, but acquiesced.

"I, uh, just came to tell you that I'm gonna go by the hospital and see Mya." He sat next to Sydney and put a palm on her covered thigh.

"I have to tell ya, I'm not sure about her," Sydney said. Seeking more of a connection, she placed her hand on top of his. She hadn't seen Anthony since last night. She'd briefly fed from him, without much interaction. It was only later that Kade had told her what he'd done to save him.

"From my perspective, she was in cahoots with Pat and Dominique," Kade speculated. "Granted, I never once saw her downstairs. But I never saw Dominique either."

"Yeah, I dunno. She was loaded up with H," Anthony added. Preliminary blood tests had shown she'd been injected with heroin. "But the docs say she's not an addict. Whatever she had in her, she'd been given in the past forty-eight hours."

"When I met her, she seemed so…I don't know…innocent. I guess my instincts were way off. She did hesitate when she shot me, and the way Pat talked about her, it was as if he knew her."

"Well, we got her covered down at the hospital. The docs called me and said she's coming round. She's starting to talk. I'll go see what she has to say. Given the crime scene in her apartment and indications of possible sexual assault, the DA's probably gonna let her go," Anthony guessed.

"But what if it was staged?" Kade protested.

"What if it wasn't?" he countered. "She was on drugs. With the amount she had in her, coupled with the apparent torture, I don't know. I, of all people, would like to see her go down after what she did to Sydney, but I saw those burns on her neck. I can't imagine her letting someone do that to her willingly. She was barely alive."

"I'll give you all a call when I find out more. So, uh, I was thinking…" Anthony paused, his eyes locked on Sydney's. "You gonna be okay? I mean, I can take some time off if you need me. I kind of wanted to stick around and wrap things up with this case anyway."

"Yeah, I'm fine…thanks to you. You saved me. Saved us." Sydney sat up and kissed his cheek once, her lips inches from his. She turned and smiled at Kade who sensed her arousal. She knew she'd never make love to Anthony, nor would she love him, but if he was willing, she knew for certain, they'd feed with him again. "We'd love to have you stay with us. You're always welcome in our home."

"Did he tell you what he did to me?" Anthony blushed and leaned back onto the heels of his hands.

"He told me you saved him. And for that I'm very, very grateful." She smiled.

"So am I. There's no way we can repay you for what you did," Kade added.

"You don't have to. We're friends. But I meant what I said last night. I'm not going with Luca again. He's kind of a dick."

"Yeah, he can be." Kade laughed.

"He's, um, difficult to get to know," Sydney offered. "Especially when you're a human. You have to give him time to warm up to you."

"Yeah, I can see him warmin' up all right. And then bitin' me like a police dog. No thanks." Anthony stood and brushed his palms down his slacks. "Your girl there seems to have tamed him. You should have seen her barkin' out orders before we went in. She told him right then she was going in alone."

"Yeah, about that," Kade growled. A dangerous smile crossed his face.

Sydney's heart stopped, aware that he was about to do something she might not like.

"Listen, sounds like you two have somethin' to work out. I'll see you guys later. Have fun, Syd." Anthony winked and walked out the bedroom.

"What?" Sydney laughed. "What did I do?"

Kade stripped back the sheets. Gooseflesh rippled across Sydney's exposed skin. The cool air was tempered by the heat that grew between her legs. Like wild prey, she froze. Unsure what he'd do, she tensed in anticipation. A gasp escaped her lips as he reached for her waist, dragging her torso across his legs. Her cheek brushed the soft cotton and she gave a nervous laugh.

"What are you doing? Ahh…" She squirmed as the light touch of his fingers grazed over her hair, trailing between her shoulder blades and onto the small of her back.

"You are a naughty vampire." His hand continued further over her buttocks to the back of her thigh.

"Maybe I like being wicked." She kicked her feet, feigning escape.

"Do you now?" His cock grew thick against the side of her belly.

"Yes, I do. Are you planning on doing something about it?" she goaded. As she went to move, he pressed a firm hand to her shoulder, pinning her still.

"I've been looking forward to this ever since you ran from me back to Philadelphia," he said, a dark tone to his voice. "Then you ran a second time to Embo. And going into danger alone…without Luca? I'm afraid you need a lesson."

"Looking forward to what? Ow…ah," she cried as a hard slap landed on her bottom. *Holy hell.* He'd teased her for months that he'd spank her. He'd even bound her to the bed on occasion, yet the sting of his palm came as an erotic surprise.

"You see," he said, smacking the other cheek. "I know you better than you know yourself. The rush you get from the danger. How do you like it now, my little vamp?"

"I don't know…I…" The wetness in her swollen folds dripped down her thigh and she attempted to conceal her arousal with words. "I don't like…"

He slapped her hard, caressing her reddened flesh. Sydney reached for his cock and swiped her finger across its wet slit. Her ass tingled in sweet pain, yet as she yearned for more, he stopped. She'd hoped that he'd continue, and was taken by surprise when his fingers glided down her crevice. A thick digit plunged deep inside her pussy and she moaned, pressing back into the erotic invasion. Retreating, he coated his fingers in her wetness and entered her again, this time circling her puckered flesh with his thumb.

"Oh God, Kade...what are you...?" With the shock of the intrusion, her fingers loosened around his dick. Unable to move, she did nothing...only felt, immersing herself in the sensation her mate sought to give her.

"You may be a novice, love, but I am a master," he told her.

"Ah...yes." He continued to tease her bottom as his remaining fingers scissored around her swollen lips, pinching her clit, never actually touching her taut nub. Her clit ached in arousal. "I need more...I need..."

"No more running."

"No, no, no," she protested as he removed his fingers from inside her. She gave a muffled whine into the covers. Her hips pumped against his legs seeking relief, but none came. "Ahh...I'm so close."

"I love your body," he said softly. "I love all of you."

"Don't stop..." She grew dizzy with need, his fingers brushing over her clitoris.

"You're so fucking wet." Entering her once again, he allowed the tip of his thumb to press gently into her anus.

"Yes...that feels...it's so wrong, but oh my God. Kade...easy...oh, yes...ah," she cried.

Quivering, her climax slammed into her. Tears

brimmed from her lashes as she began to shake. Her fingers fisted his cock as she writhed against his hand. As the spasms subsided, she pushed onto her elbows and knees. Her tousled hair flew in all directions as she whirled between his legs.

Never releasing his swollen flesh, she returned his devious smile as she dipped her head and brought her lips to his cock. Her tongue darted out and lapped at his salty essence. She licked underneath his hard length, and he groaned, hitting his head upon the headboard. Sydney laughed at his response, knowing that despite his declaration that he was the master, she'd mastered him as well. Taking him into her mouth, she sucked and laved at his soft skin. Clutching his hips, she swallowed him down to his root.

His fingers raked into her scalp, guiding her up and down. He lasted only minutes before stopping her, lifting her chin to meet his gaze.

"Come to me," he directed, wiping her lip with his thumb.

She did as he said, climbing atop her mate. Grazing her hands down his ripped abs, she hovered above him, his tip prodding her entrance. He gave her a wicked smile and flipped her onto her back. She squealed in delight as he pinned her arms to the bed.

"Make love to me," she whispered. Her quickening breath struggled to keep up with her heartbeat. She knew what was coming but nothing ever prepared her for his possession.

"For the rest of your life," he promised.

She gasped as he pushed deep inside her, his thick flesh stretching her. As he filled her, she clutched at his shoulders, her fangs dropping. She reveled in the sharp penetration, the walls of her core clamping down around his shaft. He rocked inside her, taking her pink nipple between his lips. Her hips met his, thrust for thrust, his pelvis stroking her clit in a tantalizing rhythm. His sharp teeth descended, piercing her full breast.

An orgasm rolled through her as he sucked her gently. Never giving her quarter, he increased his pace. She rebounded from her climax only to be driven to the precipice of ecstasy once again.

"Kade!" Her head thrashed on the pillow as she screamed.

He bit at her lips, silencing her with his savage kiss. She gave back what she got, biting, their tongues probing each other's. He pounded into her and she rose to meet his need. Moving to accept his cock, she lifted her hips. As he slammed into Sydney, her pussy pulsated around his length. Only the taste of her mate would suffice, and she sought to give him the pleasure he'd given her hundreds of times. He closed the distance, offering her his neck. Without hesitation, she bit down, her fangs slicing into his taut flesh. His powerful blood rushed down her throat, and she came hard, her body shuddering in release.

Kade cried out loud, his explosive orgasm blasting through him. He ground his body against hers. Erupting inside her, he surged into climax. As she laved at the wounds on his skin, he rolled onto his back, never letting her go.

For two hundred years, he'd been alone, and he'd almost lost the love of his life. Two hearts had once again been brought together. The death of her humanity brought to life again, reaffirming their commitment. As she fell asleep on his chest, the emotion he'd held at bay surfaced. He'd never been more grateful for what he'd been given: his soon-to-be wife, a future family. For eternity, they'd be lost in each other's embrace.

❧ *Epilogue* ❧

Mya smiled as the elevator numbers ticked by above her. She'd easily bypassed the detective in the hospital, her appearance once again altered to suit her purpose. Her only regret was allowing Pat to suck her into his epic fail of a plan to kill Sydney Willows. Not only had she lived, they'd been forced to kidnap the redheaded vampire. Hostages were always a burden. With her still alive, she'd have to deal with her sometime.

Mya reached underneath the floral silk scarf tied stylishly around her neck and fingered the newly healed scabs. She supposed that receiving pain could be a means to an end. A shame it hadn't played out the way Pat had wanted. Mya never played the victim well, though. Pat had known it when he'd asked for her help. She laughed to herself, knowing full well that her sadistic nature would always take precedence over any man's desire to bend her.

As the doors slid open, she smiled. Her plane ride had been filled with delightful dreams of pain. Some would call them nightmares. She'd call them a wet dream laced in blood. She reveled in the fear, excited to share it with her victims.

In truth, they got what they deserved. Nothing was ever as simple as it seemed. No one was one hundred percent innocent nor were they guilty. The spectrum of evil was as wide as the ocean, its waves readying to drown those who stood in its path.

Katrina Livingston, sister of Tristan, Alpha of Lyceum Wolves, would suffer greatly for the sins of others and perhaps her own. Within minutes, Mya would have her to do with as she pleased. As she exited and rolled her red leather carry-on down the hallway, she considered the implements of pain she'd packed for her session.

It only took her seconds to reach the young wolf's apartment. *It's entertaining to play with wolves*, she mused. Vampires were far too easy to kill, taking the thrill out of the hunt. She reached for the welcome heart that hung on the door, tracing her fingers over the last name: *Livingston*. All was well with her life.

With the excitement of New Orleans, she'd almost forgotten her commitment to her new project. She would have loved to have stayed in the south a bit longer. A shame, really, that she'd been caught by the detective.

Her phone buzzed, and she retrieved her purse to view the text message. Pleased, she glanced at the photo and smiled. His caretakers had seen that he stayed just how she'd left him, bound naked in the dark.

She could have left him for weeks, she knew. Immortality was a delicious benefit when torturing supernaturals. Whether it be for revenge or pleasure, with nothing but time, she'd always met her goals, carrying out her devious plans at her leisure. She glanced at the image again, sliding her fingers across the glass to enlarge it. A tingle of delight shivered through her body as she studied his face. His blond hair had grown longer. Through the waterfall of strands covering his face, she could taste the anger emanating from his eyes. She smiled, delighted she'd elicited her intended response.

Unfazed by the Alpha's obvious discomfort, she tossed her cell in her purse. The big bad wolf, Jax Chandler, could wait a bit longer. She knocked on the door, adrenaline rushing through her veins. *Let the fun begin.*

Erotic Romance by Kym Grosso

The Immortals of New Orleans

Kade's Dark Embrace
(Immortals of New Orleans, Book 1)

Luca's Magic Embrace
(Immortals of New Orleans, Book 2)

Tristan's Lyceum Wolves
(Immortals of New Orleans, Book 3)

Logan's Acadian Wolves
(Immortals of New Orleans, Book 4)

Léopold's Wicked Embrace
(Immortals of New Orleans, Book 5)

Dimitri
(Immortals of New Orleans, Book 6)

Lost Embrace
(Immortals of New Orleans, Book 6.5)

Jax's Story
(Immortals of New Orleans, Book 7)
Coming Fall 2015

About the Author

Kym Grosso is the USA Today bestselling and award-winning author of the erotic romance series, *The Immortals of New Orleans and Club Altura*. In addition to romance, Kym has written and published several articles about autism, and is a contributing essay author in *Chicken Soup for the Soul: Raising Kids on the Spectrum*.

Kym lives with her family in Pennsylvania, and her hobbies include reading, tennis, zumba, and spending time with her husband and children. She loves traveling just about anywhere that has a beach or snow-covered mountains. New Orleans, with its rich culture, history and unique cuisine, is one of her favorite places to visit.

• • • •

Social Media/Links:

Website: http://www.KymGrosso.com
Facebook: http://www.facebook.com/KymGrossoBooks
Twitter: https://twitter.com/KymGrosso
Pinterest: http://www.pinterest.com/kymgrosso/

Sign up for Kym's Newsletter to get Updates and Information about New Releases:
http://www.kymgrosso.com/members-only

Made in the USA
San Bernardino, CA
22 July 2016